A PENGUIN

INSPECTOR CADAVER

GEORGES JOSEPH CHRISTIAN SIMENON was born on February 12, 1903, in Liège, Belgium. He began work as a reporter for a local newspaper at the age of sixteen, and at nineteen he moved to Paris to embark on a career as a novelist. He started by writing pulp-fiction novels and novellas published, under various pseudonyms, from 1923 onwards. He went on to write seventy-five Maigret novels and twenty-eight Maigret short stories.

Although Simenon is best known in Britain as the writer of the Maigret books, his prolific output of over four hundred novels made him a household name and institution in Continental Europe, where much of his work is constantly in print. The dark realism of Simenon's books has lent them naturally to screen adaptation.

Simenon died in 1989 in Lausanne, Switzerland, where he had lived for the latter part of his life.

GEORGES SIMENON

INSPECTOR CADAVER

TRANSLATED BY
HELEN THOMSON

PENGUIN BOOKS

PENGUIN BOOKS

Published by the Penguin Group

Penguin Group (USA) Inc., 375 Hudson Street, New York, New York 10014, U.S.A.
Penguin Group (Canada), 90 Eglinton Avenue East, Suite 700, Toronto,
Ontario, Canada M4P 2Y3 (a division of Pearson Penguin Canada Inc.)
Penguin Books Ltd, 80 Strand, London WC2R 0RL, England
Penguin Ireland, 25 St Stephen's Green, Dublin 2, Ireland
(a division of Penguin Books Ltd)
Penguin Group (Australia), 250 Camberwell Road, Camberwell,
Victoria 3124, Australia (a division of Pearson Australia Group Pty Ltd)
Penguin Books India Pvt Ltd, 11 Community Centre,
Panchsheel Park, New Delhi – 110 017, India
Penguin Group (NZ), 67 Apollo Drive, Rosedale, North Shore 0632,
New Zealand (a division of Pearson New Zealand Ltd)
Penguin Books (South Africa) (Pty) Ltd, 24 Sturdee Avenue,
Rosebank, Johannesburg 2196, South Africa

Penguin Books Ltd, Registered Offices:
80 Strand, London WC2R 0RL, England

First published as *L'Inspecteur cadavre* 1944
This translation first published as *Maigret's Rival* by Hamish Hamilton 1979
Reissued under the present title, with minor revisions and
a new introduction in Penguin Classics 2003
This edition published by Penguin Books (USA) 2007

1 3 5 7 9 10 8 6 4 2

Copyright © 1944 Georges Simenon Ltd (a Chorion company). All rights reserved.
Translation copyright © Georges Simenon Ltd, 1979, 2003
All rights reserved

LIBRARY OF CONGRESS CATALOGING IN PUBLICATION DATA
Simenon, Georges, 1903–1989.
[Inspecteur Cadavre, English]
Inspector Cadaver / Georges Simenon ; translated by Helen Thomson.
p.   cm.—(A Penguin mystery)
ISBN 978-0-14-311281-5
1. Maigret, Jules (Fictitious character)—Fiction.   2. Police—France—Paris—Fiction.
3. Paris (France)—Fiction.   I. Thomson, Helen, 1945–   II. Title.
PQ2637.I53I613   2008
843'.912—dc22   2007025934

Printed in the United States of America

CONTENTS

THE LITTLE EVENING TRAIN

Maigret surveyed his fellow passengers with large, sullen eyes and, without meaning to, assumed that stuck-up, self-important look people put on when they have spent mindless hours in the compartment of a train. Then, well before the train began to slow down as it approached a station, men in large, billowing overcoats started to emerge from their various cells each clutching a leather briefcase or a suitcase, in order to take up their positions in the corridor. There they stood, one hand casually gripping the brass rod across the window, without apparently paying the slightest attention to their traveling companions.

Huge raindrops were making horizontal streaks across this particular train window. Through the transparent, watery glass the superintendent saw the light from a signal box shatter into a thousand pointed beams, for it was now dark. Lower down, he glimpsed streets laid out in straight lines, glistening like canals, rows of houses which all looked exactly the same, windows, doorsteps, pavements and, in the midst of this universe, a solitary human figure, a man in a hooded cloak hurrying somewhere or other.

Slowly and carefully, Maigret filled his pipe. In order to light it, he turned towards the procession of people in the corridor. Four or five passengers who, like himself, were waiting for the train to stop so that they could slip away into the deserted streets or quickly make their way to the station buffet, were standing between him and the end of the corridor. Among them, he recognized a pale face which immediately turned the other way.

It was none other than old Cadaver!

First of all, the superintendent groaned:

"He's pretended not to see me, the idiot."

Then he frowned. Why on earth would Inspector Cavre be going to Saint-Aubin-les-Marais?

The train slowed down and pulled into Niort station. Maigret stepped on to the cold and wet platform and called a porter:

"Can you tell me how to get to Saint-Aubin, please?"

"Take the 20:17 train on platform 3 . . ."

He had half an hour to wait. After a brief visit to the gentlemen's lavatory, which was right at the end of the platform, he pushed open the door of the station buffet and walked over to one of the many unoccupied tables. He then sat wearily on a chair and settled down to wait in the dusty light.

Old Cadaver was there, at the other end of the room, sitting as Maigret was, at a table with no cloth on it, and once again he pretended he had not seen the superintendent.

Cavre was his real name, Justin Cavre, but he had been known as old Cadaver for twenty years and everyone at the Police Judiciaire used this nickname when referring to him.

He looked ridiculous sitting stiffly in his corner and shifting from one uncomfortable position to another in order not to catch Maigret's eye. He knew the superintendent had seen him, that was certain. Skinny, sallow-skinned, his eyelids red, he made one think of those schoolboys who skulk peevishly at the edge of the play-ground and pretend they do not want to play with the rest of the class, although in reality they long to join in the fun.

Cavre was just that sort of person. He was intelligent. He was probably the most intelligent man Maigret had come across in the police force. They were both about the same age. If the truth were known, Cavre was a little more experienced and, had he persevered, he could well have become a superintendent before Maigret.

Why was it that even as a young man he already seemed to carry the burden of some kind of curse on his narrow shoulders? Why did he give them all black looks, as if he thought each and every one of them was going to do him down?

"Old Cadaver has just begun his novena . . ."

It was an expression one often used to hear at the Quai des Orfèvres years ago. At the slightest provocation, or sometimes for no reason at all, Inspector Cavre would suddenly begin a course of silence and mistrust, a restorative of hatred, one might say. For a week at a time he would not say a word to anyone. Sometimes, his colleagues would catch sight of him chuckling to himself as though he had seen through their supposedly evil schemes.

Very few people knew why he had suddenly left the police force. Maigret himself did not learn the facts until some time afterwards and had felt very sorry for him.

Cavre loved his wife with the jealous, consuming passion of a lover rather than in a husbandly way. What exactly he found so beguiling about that vulgar woman who had all the aggressive characteristics of a *demi-mondaine* or a bogus film star, one could only surmise. Nevertheless, the fact remained that it was because of her that he had committed serious offenses in the course of his career in the force. Ugly discoveries concerning payments of money had sealed his fate. One evening, Cavre had emerged from the Chief of Police's office with his head down and his shoulders hunched. A few months later, he was known to have set up a private detective agency above a stamp shop in the Rue Drouot.

People were having dinner, each customer wrapped in his own aura of boredom and silence. Maigret finished his half pint of beer, wiped his mouth, picked up his suitcase and walked past his former colleague. He had been less than two yards away from his table, but Cavre had continued to stare down at a patch of spit on the floor.

The little train, looking black and wet, was already at platform 3. Maigret climbed into a cold, damp compartment of the old-fashioned type and tried in vain to shut the window properly.

People were walking to and fro on the platform outside and the superintendent heard other familiar sounds. The carriage door opened two or three times and a head looked in. Each passenger was trying desperately to find an empty compartment. Whenever one of them caught sight of Maigret, the door shut again.

Once the train had started to move, the superintendent went out into the corridor to close a window which was causing a draft. As he did so, he saw, in the compartment next to his, Inspector Cavre, who this time was pretending to be asleep.

There was nothing to be alarmed about. It was idiotic to keep brooding on this strange coincidence. Besides, the whole affair was nonsense and Maigret wished he could extricate himself from his promise with a mere shrug of the shoulders.

What difference did it make to him if Cavre was also going to Saint-Aubin?

In the darkness outside the carriage windows, through which the dot of a light on the side of the road could occasionally be seen, the headlights of a passing car would flash by or, looking even more mysterious and inviting, the yellowish rectangle of a window.

The examining magistrate Bréjon, a charming, good-natured, rather shy man full of old-world courtesy, had repeatedly said to him:

"My brother-in-law Naud will meet you at the station. I've told him you're coming."

And Maigret could not help thinking as he drew on his pipe: "But what on earth can old Cadaver be up to?"

The superintendent was not even on an official case. Bréjon, with whom he had worked so often, had sent him a short note asking him if he would be good enough to pop into his office for a few moments.

It was the month of January. It was raining in Paris as it was in Niort. It had been raining for more than a week and the sun had not once come out. The lamp on the desk in the examining magistrate's office had a green shade. While Monsieur Bréjon was talking and constantly cleaning the lenses of his spectacles as he did so, Maigret reflected that he, too, had a green lampshade in his office, but that the one he was looking at now was ribbed like a melon.

". . . am so sorry to bother you . . . especially as it's not a professional matter . . . Do sit down . . . But of course . . . A cigar? . . . You may perhaps know that my wife's maiden name is Lecat . . . It doesn't matter . . . That's not what I want to discuss . . . My sister, Louise Bréjon, became Madame Naud when she married . . ."

It was late. People in the street outside, on looking up

at the gloomy façade of the forbidding Palais de Justice and seeing the light on in the examining magistrate's office, would no doubt think that serious issues were being debated up there.

And one had such a strong impression of authority when one saw Maigret's bulky figure and thoughtful countenance that no one could possibly have guessed what he was thinking about.

In actual fact, as he listened with half an ear to what the examining magistrate with the goatee beard was telling him, he was thinking about the green lampshade in front of him, about the one in his own office, how attractive the ribbed shade was, and how he would get one like it for himself.

"You can understand the situation . . . A small, a tiny village . . . You will see for yourself . . . It's miles from anywhere . . . The jealousy, the envy, the unwarranted malice . . . My brother-in-law is a charming person, and sincere too . . . As for my niece, she's just a child . . . If you agree, I'll arrange for you to have a week's leave of absence. My entire family will be indebted to you, and . . . and . . ."

That was how he had become involved in a stupid venture. What exactly *had* the little examining magistrate told him? He was still provincial in his outlook and like all provincials he let himself be carried away by local gossip about families whose names he pronounced as if they were of historical importance.

His sister, Louise Bréjon, had married Etienne

Naud. The examining magistrate had added, as if the whole world had heard of him:

"The son of Sébastien Naud, you understand?"

Now, Sébastien Naud was quite simply a stout cattle dealer from the village of Saint-Aubin which was tucked away in the heart of the Vendée fenland.

"Etienne Naud is related, on his mother's side, to the best families in the district."

That was all very well. But what of it?

"They live about a mile outside the village and their house almost touches the railway line . . . the one that runs between Niort and Fontenay-le-Comte . . . About three weeks ago, a local boy—from quite a good family, too, at any rate on his mother's side as she's a Pelcau— was found dead on the tracks . . . At first, everybody thought it was an accident, and I still think it was . . . But since then, rumor has it . . . Anonymous letters have been sent around . . . In a nutshell, my brother-in-law is now in a terrible state as people are accusing him almost openly of having killed the boy . . . He wrote me a somewhat garbled letter about it . . . I then wrote to the Director of Public Prosecutions in Fontenay-le-Comte for more detailed information, as Saint-Aubin comes under the jurisdiction of Fontenay. Contrary to what I expected, I discovered that the accusations were rather serious and that it will be difficult to avoid an official inquiry . . . That is why, my dear superintendent, I have taken it upon myself to contact you, purely as a friend . . ."

The train stopped. Maigret wiped the condensation from the window and saw a tiny station with just one light, one platform and one solitary railwayman who was running along the side of the train and already blowing his whistle. A carriage door slammed shut and the train set off again. But it was not the door of the next-door compartment which Maigret had heard closing. Inspector Cavre was still there.

Now and then, Maigret would glimpse a farm, near by or in the distance, but always beneath him as he peered through the window, and whenever he saw a light it would invariably be reflected in a pool of water, as if the train were skirting the edge of a lake.

"Saint-Aubin!"

He got out. Three people in all got off the train: a very old lady with a cumbersome, black wicker basket, Cavre and Maigret. In the middle of the platform stood a very tall, very large man, wearing leather gaiters and a leather jacket. It was obviously Naud, for he was looking hesitantly about him. His brother-in-law the examining magistrate had told him Maigret would be arriving that night. But which of the two men who had got out of the train was Maigret?

First of all, he walked towards the thinner of the two men. His hand was already moving upwards to touch his hat; his mouth was slightly open, ready to ask the stranger's name in a faltering voice. But Cavre walked straight past, haughtily, as if to say with a knowing look:

"It's not me. It's the other chap."

The examining magistrate's brother-in-law abruptly changed direction.

"Superintendent Maigret, I believe? I'm sorry I did not recognize you straightaway. Your photograph is so often in the papers. But in this little backwater, you know . . ."

He had taken it upon himself to carry Maigret's suitcase and as the superintendent was hunting in his pocket for his ticket, he said as he steered him, not towards the station exit but towards the level crossing:

"Don't worry about that . . ."

And turning to the station master, he cried:

"Good evening, Pierre . . ."

It was still raining. A horse harnessed to a pony trap was tied to a ring.

"Please climb up . . . The road is virtually impassable for cars in this weather."

Where was Cavre? Maigret had seen him disappear into the darkness. He had a strong desire to follow him, but it was too late. Moreover, would it not have looked extremely odd, so soon upon his arrival, to leave his host in the lurch and go off in hot pursuit of another passenger?

There was no sign of an actual village. Just a single lamp-post about a hundred yards from the station, standing by some tall trees. At this point, a road seemed to open out.

"Put the coat over your legs. Yes, you must. Even with the coat your knees will get wet, for we're going against the wind . . . My brother-in-law wrote me a long letter all about you . . . I feel embarrassed that he has involved someone like you in such an unimportant matter . . . You have no idea what country folk are like . . ."

He let the end of his whip dangle over the horse's rump. The wheels of the pony trap sank deep into the black mud as they drove along the road which ran parallel to the railway line. On the other side, lanterns threw a hazy light over a kind of canal.

A human figure suddenly appeared on the road as if from nowhere. A man holding his jacket over his head moved out of the way as the pony trap came nearer.

"Good evening, Fabien!" cried out Etienne Naud in the same way as he had hailed the station master, like a country squire who calls everyone by his Christian name, a man who knows everyone in the neighborhood.

But where the devil could Cavre be? Try as he might to put the matter out of his mind, Maigret could think of nothing else.

"Is there a hotel in Saint-Aubin?" he asked.

His companion roared with laughter.

"There's no question of your staying in a hotel! We have plenty of room at home. Your room is ready. We've arranged to have dinner an hour later than usual as I thought you wouldn't have had anything to eat on your journey. I hope you were wise enough not to have dinner at the station buffet in Niort? We live very simply, however . . ."

Maigret could not have cared less how they lived or what sort of welcome he received. He had Cavre on the brain.

"I'd like to know if the man who got out of the train with me . . ."

"I don't know who he was," Etienne Naud hurriedly declared.

Why did he reply in such a fashion? It was not the answer to Maigret's question.

"I'd like to know if he'll have managed to find somewhere to stay . . ."

"Indeed! I don't know what my brother-in-law has been telling you about this part of the world. Now that he's living in Paris he probably looks upon Saint-Aubin as an insignificant little hamlet. But, my dear chap, it is almost a small town. You haven't seen any of it yet because the station is a little way from the center. There are two excellent inns, the Lion d'Or, run by Monsieur Taponnier, old François as everyone calls him, and just opposite there's the Hôtel des Trois Mules . . . Well! We're nearly home . . . That light you can see . . . Yes . . . That's our humble dwelling . . ."

Needless to say, the tone of voice in which he spoke made it abundantly clear that it was a large house and, sure enough, it was a large, low, solid-looking building with the lights on in four windows on the ground floor.

Outside, in the middle of the façade, an electric lamp shone like a star and gave light to any visitor.

Behind the house, there was presumably a large courtyard with stables around the edge so that one would occasionally catch the warm, sweet smell of the horses within. A farmhand rushed up immediately to lead in the horse and trap, the door of the house opened and a maid came forward to take the traveler's luggage.

"Here we are, then! It's not very far, you see . . . At the time the house was built, no one foresaw unfortunately that the railway line would one day pass virtually beneath our windows. You get used to it, admittedly, and in fact there are very few trains, but . . . Do come in . . . Give me your coat . . ."

At that precise moment, Maigret was thinking:

"He has talked non-stop."

And then he could not think at all for a moment because too many thoughts were assailing him and a totally new atmosphere was closing in on him in an ever tighter net.

The passageway was wide and paved with gray tiles, its walls paneled in dark wood up to a height of about six feet. The electric light was enclosed in a lantern of colored glass. A large oak staircase with a red stair carpet and heavy, well-polished banisters led up to the second floor. A pleasing aroma of wax polish, of casseroles simmering in the kitchen pervaded the whole house and Maigret caught a whiff of something else too, that bittersweet smell which for him was the very essence of the country.

But the most remarkable feature of the house was its stillness, a stillness which seemed to be eternal. It was as if the furniture and every object in this house had remained in the same place for generations, as if the occupants themselves, as they went in and out of the rooms, were observing special rites which hurled defiance at anything unforeseen.

"Would you like to go up to your room for a moment before we eat? It's a family occasion, you understand. We shan't stand on ceremony . . ."

The master of the house pushed open a door and two people rose to their feet simultaneously. Maigret was ushered into a warm, homely drawing-room.

"This is Superintendent Maigret . . . My wife . . ."

She had the same deferential air about her as her brother Bréjon, the examining magistrate, the same courteousness so characteristic of a sound bourgeois upbringing, but for a second Maigret thought he detected something harder, sharper in her countenance.

"I am appalled my brother has asked you to come all this way in weather like this . . ."

As if the rain made any difference to the journey or was of any importance in the circumstances!

"May I introduce you to a friend of ours, superintendent: Alban Groult-Cotelle. I expect my brother-in-law mentioned his name to you . . ."

Had the examining magistrate mentioned him? Perhaps he had. Maigret had been so preoccupied thinking about the green ribbed lampshade!

"How do you do, superintendent. I'm a great admirer of yours . . ."

Maigret was tempted to reply:

"Well, I'm not of yours."

For he could not abide people like Groult-Cotelle.

"Would you like to serve the *porto,* Louise?"

The glasses were on a table in the drawing-room which was softly lit with few, if any, sharp lines. The chairs were old, most of them upholstered; the rugs were all in neutral or faded colors. A cat lay stretched out on the hearth in front of the log fire.

"Do sit down . . . Our neighbor Groult-Cotelle is having dinner with us . . ."

Whenever his name was mentioned, Groult-Cotelle would bow pretentiously, like a nobleman among commoners who takes it upon himself to behave as if he were in a salon.

"They insist on laying a place at their table for an old recluse like me . . ."

A recluse, yes, and probably a bachelor too. One could not say why one sensed this, but one sensed it all the same. He was stuck-up, a good-for-nothing who was well satisfied with his peculiar notions and eccentric behavior.

The fact that he was not a count or a marquis, that

he did not even have a "de" in front of his name, must have been a considerable source of annoyance. All the same, he did have an affected Christian name, Alban, which he so liked to hear, and an equally pretentious double-barreled surname to go with it.

He was a tall, lean man of about forty and he obviously thought this leanness gave him an aristocratic bearing. The dusty look he had about him, in spite of the care with which he dressed, his dull face and bald forehead gave Maigret the impression he did not have a wife. His clothes were elegant, subtle and unusual in color; seeming never to have been new, they did not look as if they would ever become old or threadbare either. The garments he wore were part of his character and never changed. Whenever Maigret met him subsequently, he would always be wearing the same greenish colored jacket, very much in the style of the country gentleman, and the same horseshoe tiepin on a white ribbed cotton tie.

"I hope the journey wasn't too tiring, superintendent?" inquired Louise Bréjon, as she handed him a glass of *porto*.

And Maigret, firmly seated in an armchair that sagged beneath his weight, much to the distress of the mistress of the house, was prey to so many different emotions that his mind became rather blunted and for part of the evening his hosts must have thought him somewhat slow-witted.

First of all, there was the house, which was the

very prototype of the house he had dreamed of so often, with its comforting walls round which hung air as thick as solid matter. The framed portraits reminded him of the examining magistrate's lengthy discourse about the Nauds, the Bréjons, the La Noues, for the Bréjons were connected with the La Noues through their mother. One would have liked to imagine that all these serious-looking and rather stiff faces were one's own ancestors.

Judging from the smells coming from the kitchen, an elaborate meal was about to be served. Someone was carefully laying the table in the dining-room next door, for the clinking of china and cut glass could be heard. In the stable, the farmhand was rubbing down the mare and two long rows of reddish-brown cows were chewing the cud in their stalls.

The house embodied the peace of God, order and virtue, and at the same time was the very expression of the petty habits and faults of simple families living encompassed lives.

Etienne Naud, tall and broad-shouldered, with a ruddy complexion and goggle eyes, looked cordially round him as if to say:

"Look at me! . . . Sincere . . . kind . . ."

The good-natured giant. The perfect master of the house. The perfect father. The man who cried out from his pony trap:

"Good evening, Pierre . . . Good evening, Fabien . . ."

His wife smiled shyly in the shadow of the huge fellow, as if to apologize for his taking up so much space.

"Will you forgive me for a moment, superintendent . . ."

Of course. He had been expecting it. The charming mistress of the house always goes into the kitchen to have a last look at the preparations for dinner.

Even Alban Groult-Cotelle was predictable. Looking as if he had just stepped out of an engraving, he was the very picture of the more refined, the better-bred, the more intelligent friend, indeed the epitome of the old family friend with his faintly condescending airs.

"You see . . ." was written all over his face. "They're decent people, perfect neighbors . . . You can't talk philosophy with them, but apart from that, they make you feel very much at home and you'll see their Burgundy is genuine enough and their brandy worth praising . . ."

"Dinner is served, madame . . ."

"Would you like to sit on my right, superintendent? . . ."

But where was the note of anxiety in all this? For the examining magistrate had certainly been very concerned when he sent for Maigret.

"You see," he insisted, "I know my brother-in-law, just as I know my sister and niece. Anyway, you'll see them for yourself . . . But all this doesn't alter the fact that this odious accusation is increasing in substance day by day, to the point of forcing the Department of the Public Prosecutor to investigate the matter. My father was the notary in Saint-Aubin for forty years, having taken over the practice from *his* father . . . They'll show you our family house in the middle of the town . . . I have got to the stage where I ask myself how such a blind hatred could have arisen in so short a time. It is steadily gaining ground and is threatening to wreck the lives of innocent people . . . My sister has never been very robust . . . She's highly-strung and suffers from insomnia. The slightest problem upsets her."

But one would never have guessed that the people present were involved in such a drama. Everything led one to believe that Maigret had merely been asked to a good dinner and a game of bridge. While the skylarks were being served, the superintendent's hosts explained at great length how the peasants from the fens caught them at night by dragging nets over the meadows.

But why was their daughter not there?

"My niece, Geneviève," the examining magistrate had said, "is a perfect young lady, the like of which you only read about in novels now . . ."

This was not, however, what the person or persons writing the anonymous letters thought, nor for that matter what most of the locals thought, for it was Geneviève they were accusing, after all.

Maigret was still puzzled by the story he had heard from Bréjon, for it was so out of keeping with the scene before him! Rumor had it that Albert Retailleau, the young man found dead on the railway line, was Geneviève's lover. It was even said that he came to her house two or three times a week and spent the night in her room.

Albert had no money. He was barely twenty years old. His father had worked in the Saint-Aubin dairy and had died as a result of a boiler exploding. His mother lived on a pension which the dairy had been obliged to give her in recompense.

"Albert Retailleau did not commit suicide," declared his friends. "He enjoyed the pleasures of life too much. And even if he had been drunk, as is claimed to be the case, he would not have been so stupid as to cross the railway line when a train was coming."

The body had been found more than five hundred yards away from the Nauds' house, about halfway between it and the station.

There was nothing wrong in that, but it was now rumored that the boy's cap had been found in the reeds along the edge of the canal, much nearer the Nauds' house.

There was yet another, even more doubtful story in circulation. It seemed that someone had visited Madame Retailleau, the mother of the boy, a week after her son's death, and had apparently seen her hurriedly hide a wad of 1,000-franc notes. She had never been known to have such a large sum of money before.

"It is a pity, superintendent, that you have made your first visit to our part of the world in wintertime . . . It is so pretty around here in the summer that the district is known as 'Green Venice' . . . You'll have some more of the pullet, won't you?"

And Cavre? What was Inspector Cavre up to in Saint-Aubin?

Everyone ate and drank too much. It was too hot in the dining-room. Sluggishly, they all returned to the drawing-room and sat around the crackling log fire.

"I insist . . . I know you're particularly fond of your pipe, but you must have a cigar . . ."

Were they trying to lull him to sleep? But that was a ridiculous thought. They were decent sorts. That was all there was to it. The examining magistrate in Paris must have exaggerated the situation. And Alban Groult-Cotelle was nothing but a stuck-up fool, one of those dandyish good-for-nothings to be found in any country district.

"You must be tired after your journey . . . Just say when you want to go to bed . . ."

That meant that nothing was going to be said that night. Perhaps because Groult-Cotelle was there? Or because Naud preferred not to say anything in front of his wife?

"Do you take coffee at night? . . . No? . . . No tisane either? . . . Please forgive me if I go up now, but our daughter hasn't been very well for the past two or three days and I must go and see if she needs anything . . . Young girls are always rather delicate, aren't they, especially in a climate like ours . . ."

The three men sat around the fire smoking and talking of this and that. They even began discussing local politics, for apparently there was a new mayor who was acting counter to the wishes of all respectable members of the community and who . . .

"Well gentlemen," grunted Maigret finally, half-pleasantly, half-crossly, "if you will excuse me, I think I'll go up to bed now . . ."

"You must sleep the night here, too, Alban . . . I'm not going to let you go home in this terrible weather . . ."

They went upstairs. Maigret's room was at the end of the passageway. Its walls were covered in yellow cloth and brought back many childhood memories.

"Have you everything you need? . . . I forgot . . . Let me show you the bathroom."

Maigret shook hands with the two men, then undressed and got into bed. As he lay there half-asleep, he thought he heard noises, the distant murmur of voices somewhere in the house, but soon, when all the lights were out, these sounds died away.

He fell asleep. Or he thought he did. The sinister face of Cavre, that most unhappy of men, kept creeping into his unconscious, and then he dreamt that the rosy-cheeked maid who served the dinner was bringing him his breakfast.

The door half-opened. He was sure he heard the door open gently. He sat up in bed and groped for the switch to the light bulb in the tulip-shaped opal glass covering attached to the wall above the bedhead. The light went on and Maigret saw standing in front of him a young girl with a brown wool coat over her nightdress.

"Ssh . . ." she whispered. "I just had to speak to you. Don't make a noise . . ."

And, like a sleepwalker, she sat down on a chair and stared into space.

2

THE GIRL IN THE NIGHTDRESS

It was a weary night for Maigret, and yet not without its enjoyment. He slept without sleeping. He dreamed without dreaming, or in other words he was well aware he was dreaming and deliberately prolonged his dreams, being conscious all the time of noises from the real world.

For example, the sound of the mare kicking her hooves against the stable wall was real enough, but the other images that flitted through Maigret's mind, as he lay in bed perspiring heavily, were tricks of the imagination. He conjured up a picture of the dim light in a stable, the horse's rump, the rack half full of hay; he imagined the rain still falling in the courtyard with figures splashing their way through black puddles of water and lastly he saw, from the outside, the house in which he was staying.

It was a kind of double vision. He was in his bed. He was keenly savoring its warmth and the delicious country smell of the mattress which became even more pungent as it grew moist with Maigret's sweat. But at the same time he was in the whole house. Who knows if, at one moment in his dream, he did not even become the house itself?

Throughout the night, he was conscious of the cows moving about in their stalls, and from four in the morning onwards he heard the footsteps of a farmhand crossing the courtyard and the sound of the latch being lifted: what prevented him from actually seeing the man, by the light of a hurricane lamp, as he sat on a three-legged stool drawing milk into white metal buckets?

He must have fallen into a deep sleep again, for he woke up with a start at the sound of the lavatory flushing. It was such a sudden, violent noise that it gave him rather a fright. But immediately afterwards he was back to his old tricks and imagined the master of the house coming out of the bathroom with his braces round his thighs and going silently back to his room. Madame Naud was asleep, or pretending to be, with her face to the wall. Etienne Naud had left the room in darkness except for the small wall light above the dressing-table. He started to shave, his fingers numbed by the icy water. His skin was pink, taut and glossy.

Then he sat down in an armchair to pull on his boots. Just as he was leaving the room, a sound came from beneath the blankets. What was his wife saying to him? He bent over her and murmured something in a low voice. He closed the door noiselessly behind him and tiptoed down the stairs. At this point, Maigret jumped out of bed and switched on the light, for he had had enough of these spellbinding nocturnal activities.

He looked at his watch which he had left on the bedside table. It was half past five. He listened carefully and decided that either it had stopped raining or the rain had turned into a fine, silent drizzle.

Admittedly, he had eaten and drunk well the previous evening, but he had not drunk too much. And yet this morning he felt as if he had drunk a great deal. As he took various things out of his dressing-case, he looked with heavy, swollen eyes at his unmade bed and in particular at that chair beside it.

He was convinced it had not been a dream: Geneviève Naud had come into his room. She had come in without knocking. She had positioned herself on that chair, sitting bolt upright without touching the back of it. At first, as he stared at her in sheer amazement, he had thought she was deranged. In reality, however, Maigret was infinitely more disturbed than she was. For he had never been in such a delicate situation. Never before had a young girl who was ready to pour out her heart stationed herself at his bedside, with him in bed in his nightshirt, his hair ruffled by the pillow and his lips moist with spittle.

He had muttered something like:

"If you'll turn the other way for a moment, I'll get up and put some clothes on . . ."

"It doesn't matter . . . I have only a few words to say to you . . . I am pregnant by Albert Retailleau . . . If my father finds out I'll kill myself and no one will stop me . . ."

He could not bring himself to look at her while he was lying in bed. She paused for a moment, as if expecting Maigret to react to her pronouncement, then rose to her feet, listened at the door and said as she left the room:

"Do as you wish. I am in your hands."

Even now, he could scarcely believe all this had happened and the thought that he had lain prostrate like a dummy throughout the proceedings humiliated him. He was not vain in the way men can be, and yet he was ashamed that a young girl had caught him in bed with his face still bloated by sleep. And the girl's attitude to it all was even more annoying, for she had hardly glanced at him. She had not pleaded with him, as he might have expected, she had not thrown herself at his feet, she had not wept.

He recalled her face, its regular features making her look a little like her father. He could not have said if she was beautiful but she had left him with an impression of completeness and poise which even her insane overture had not dispelled.

"I am pregnant by Albert Retailleau . . . If my father finds out I'll kill myself and no one will stop me . . ."

Maigret finished dressing and mechanically lit his first pipe of the day. He then opened the door and, failing to find the light switch, groped his way down the corridor. He went down the stairs but could not see a light on anywhere, even though he could hear someone stoking the stove. He made his way to where the noise was coming from and saw a shaft of yellow light beneath a door in the dining-room. He tapped gently on the door, opened it and found himself in the kitchen.

Etienne Naud was sitting at one end of the table, his elbows resting on the light wood, and tucking into a bowl of soup. An elderly cook in a blue apron was sending showers of white-hot cinders into the ash bucket as she raked the stove.

Maigret saw the startled look on Naud's face as he came in and realized he was annoyed at having been caught unawares in the kitchen having his breakfast like a farm worker.

"Up already, superintendent? I keep to the old country habits, you know. No matter what time I go to bed, I'm always up at five in the morning. I hope I didn't wake you?"

What was the point of telling him that it had been the sound of the lavatory flushing that had woken him up?

"I won't offer you a bowl of soup, for I presume you . . ."

"But I'd love some . . ."

"Léontine . . ."

"Yes, monsieur, I heard . . . I'll have it ready in a moment . . ."

"Did you sleep well?"

"Quite well. But at one point I thought I heard foot-steps in the passageway . . ."

Maigret brought this up in order to find out whether Naud had pounced on his daughter after she had left his room, but the look of astonishment on his face seemed genuine enough.

"When? . . . During the evening? . . . I didn't hear anything. Admittedly, it takes a lot to rouse me from my sleep early on in the night. It was probably our friend Alban getting up to go to the lavatory. What do you think of him, incidentally? A likeable fellow, isn't he? Far more cultured than he actually appears to be . . . He's read countless books, you know . . . He knows the lot, and that's about it. Pity he didn't have better luck with his wife . . ."

"He was married, then?"

Having thought Groult-Cotelle to be the archetypal bachelor living in the provinces, Maigret viewed this snippet of information somewhat suspiciously. He felt as if they had hidden something from him, as if they had deliberately tried to mislead him.

"Indeed he was, and he still is, what's more. He has two children, a girl and a boy. The elder of the two must be twelve or thirteen now . . ."

"Does his wife live with him?"

"No. She lives on the Côte d'Azur. It's rather a sad story and no one ever talks about it round here. She came from a very good family, though . . . She was a

Deharme . . . Yes, like the general . . . She's his niece. A rather eccentric woman who could never grasp the fact that she was living in Saint-Aubin and not in Paris. She scandalized the neighborhood on several occasions and then, one winter, moved to Nice, ostensibly to escape the bitter cold here, but of course she never came back. She lives there with her children . . . And she's not living alone, needless to say . . ."

"Did her husband not ask for a divorce?"

"That's not done in these parts."

"Which of them has the money?"

Etienne Naud looked at him disapprovingly, for it was obvious he did not want to go into any details.

"She is undoubtedly a very rich woman . . ."

The cook had sat down at the table to grind the coffee in an old-fashioned coffee mill with a large copper top.

"You are lucky. It has stopped raining. But my brother-in-law really ought to have told you to bring some boots. After all, he comes from this part of the world and knows it well. We are right in the middle of the fenland and even have to use a boat in summer as well as winter to reach some of my farms. They're known as *cabanes* here, by the way . . . But talking of my brother-in-law, I feel rather embarrassed he had the nerve to ask a man of your standing to . . ."

The question Maigret kept asking himself, the question that had been constantly on his mind ever since his arrival the previous evening was: were the

Nauds decent people who had nothing to hide and who were doing their utmost to make their guest from Paris feel at home, or was he in fact an unwelcome intruder whom Bréjon had deposited in their midst in a most inconsiderate fashion and whose presence this disconcerted couple could well have done without?

He decided to try an experiment.

"Not many people get off the train at Saint-Aubin," he commented as he ate his soup. "I think only two of us did yesterday, apart from the old peasant woman wearing a bonnet."

"Yes, you're right."

"Does the man who got off the train with me live around here?"

Etienne Naud hesitated before replying. Why? Maigret was looking at him so intently that he was covered in confusion.

"I'd never seen him before," he answered hurriedly. "You must have seen me dithering as to which one of you to approach . . ."

Maigret tried another tactic:

"I wonder what he has come here for, or rather who asked him to come."

"Do you know him?"

"He's a private detective. I'll have to find out where he is and what he is up to this morning. He presumably checked in at one or other of the inns you mentioned yesterday . . ."

"I'll take you into town shortly in the pony trap."

"Thanks, but I'd rather walk if you don't mind, and then I'll be free to come and go as I like . . ."

Something had just occurred to him. Supposing Naud had been counting on him to sleep soundly so that he could leave early for the village and meet Inspector Cavre?

Anything was possible here, and the superintendent even began to wonder if the young girl's appearance in his room had not been part of a plot which the whole family had planned.

A moment later, he dismissed such thoughts as foolish.

"I hope your daughter isn't seriously ill?"

"No . . . Well, if you really want the truth, I don't think she is any more ill than I am. In spite of all we've done, she has got wind of what is being said in the neighborhood. She's a proud young woman. All young women are. I'm sure that's the reason she has insisted on staying in her room for the past three days. And maybe your arrival has made her feel rather ashamed . . ."

"Ashamed, is she!" thought Maigret, as he recalled her brief appearance in his room the night before.

"We can talk in front of Léontine," Naud went on. "She's known me from childhood. She's been with the family for . . . for how many years, Léontine?"

"Ever since I took my first communion, monsieur . . ."

"A little more soup? No? . . . To continue, I'm in a

most awkward position and I sometimes think my
brother-in-law tackled the case in the wrong way. I
know you'll say he knows far more about such matters
than I do, that's his job . . . but maybe he has forgotten
what it's like in our part of the world now that he lives
in Paris . . ."

It was hard to believe he was not speaking sincerely,
for he seemed to want to talk over what was on his
mind. He sat there with his legs stretched out, filling his
pipe, while Maigret finished his breakfast. The kitchen
smelt of the freshly made coffee and the two men enjoyed the warm atmosphere of the room. Outside, in
the darkness of the courtyard, the stable hand was
whistling softly as he groomed one of the horses.

"I'll tell you straight . . . From time to time, rumors
about someone or other are spread round the town . . .
this time, it's a serious matter, I know. But I still wonder
whether it would not be wiser to disregard the accusation . . . You agreed to do what my brother-in-law
asked . . . You have done us the honor of coming . . .
Everyone knows you are here by now, that's certain.
Tongues are already wagging. No doubt you intend to
question some people and that is bound to stir their
imaginations even more . . . So that's why I really do
wonder, quite sincerely, whether we are going about
this whole business in the right way . . . Are you sure
you have had enough to eat? . . . If you don't mind the
cold, I'll be glad to show you around. I go on a tour of
inspection every morning."

Maigret was putting on his overcoat as the maid came downstairs, for she got up an hour later than the old cook. The two men went into the cold, damp courtyard and spent an hour going from one stable to another. Meanwhile, churns of milk were being loaded on to a small truck.

Some cows were going off to market in a nearby town that very day and cattle drovers in dark overalls were rounding them up. At the end of the yard was a small office with a little round stove, a table, account books and various pigeon holes inside. Sitting at the table was a farmhand wearing the same sort of boots as his boss.

"Will you excuse me a moment?"

Madame Naud was getting up now, for there was a light on in her room on the second floor. The other rooms remained in darkness which meant that Groult-Cotelle and the young girl were still fast asleep. The maid was cleaning the dining room.

Men and animals could be seen moving about in the dim light of the courtyard and outhouses, and Maigret could hear the engine of the milk truck running in the background.

"That's done . . . I was just leaving a few instructions . . . I'll be leaving by car for the market shortly as I have to meet some other farmers . . . If I had time and thought you would be interested, I would tell you how the estate is run. I have ordinary dairy cattle on my other farms, as we supply the local dairy with milk, but here we rear the finest thoroughbreds, most of which we

sell abroad . . . I even send some to South America . . .
But for the moment, I am entirely at your service . . . It
will be daylight in an hour. If you need the car . . . or if
you have any questions you would like to ask me . . . I
want you to feel at ease . . . You must treat this as your
home . . ."

His face bore a cheerful expression as he spoke, but
his smile faded when Maigret merely answered:

"Well, if you don't mind, I'll be on my way . . ."

————

The road surface was spongy, as if water from the canal
on the left had soaked the ground beneath. The railway
embankment ran along the right-hand side of the road.
About a kilometer further on, a glaring light could be
seen which was obviously the one in the station, for
there were green and red signals nearby.

Maigret looked back towards the house and saw
that there were lights on in two other windows on the
second floor. This brought Alban Groult-Cotelle into his
mind and he began to wonder why he had been so put
out to discover he was married.

The sky was brightening. One of the first houses
Maigret caught sight of as he turned to the left by the
station and approached the village bore the sign of the
Lion d'Or. The lights were on on the first floor and
he went inside. He found himself in a long, low room
where everything was brown—the walls, the beams on
the ceiling, the long polished tables and the benches with

no backs. At the very end of the room was a kitchen range which was not yet alight. A woman of indeterminate age was crouched over a log burning slowly in the hearth and waiting for the coffee to heat. She turned around for a moment to look at the stranger, but said nothing. Maigret sat down in the dim light of a very dusty lamp.

"I'd like to sample the local brandy!" he said, shaking his overcoat which the damp dawn had showered with grayish beads of moisture.

The woman did not reply and he thought she had not heard. She went on stirring the saucepan of rather uninviting coffee with her spoon and when it was to her liking she poured some into a cup, put it on a tray and walked towards the staircase.

"I'll be down in a minute," she said.

Maigret suspected that the coffee was for Cadaver, and was proved right when a few seconds later, he noticed the detective's coat hanging on the coat rack.

Footsteps sounded above Maigret's head. He could hear voices but could not make out what was being said. Five minutes went by. Then five more minutes. Every now and then Maigret rapped a coin on the wooden table, but nothing happened.

At last, a quarter of an hour later, the woman came downstairs again and spoke even less amicably than before.

"What did you say you wanted?"

"A glass of the local brandy."

"I haven't any."

"You've no brandy?"

"I've cognac, but no local brandy."

"Then give me a cognac."

She gave him a glass that had such a thick bottom that there was hardly any room for the drink.

"Tell me, madame, I believe a friend of mine arrived here last night?"

"How am I to know if he's your friend?"

"Has he just got up?"

"I have one visitor and I have just given him his coffee."

"If he's the man I know, I bet he asked you lots of questions, didn't he?"

The glasses left by the previous evening's customers had made round, wet marks on many of the tables and the woman began to wipe them with a duster.

"Albert Retailleau spent the evening here the day before he died, didn't he?"

"What's that got to do with you?"

"He was a good lad, I believe. Someone told me he played cards that evening. Is *belote* the favorite game in this part of the world?"

"No, we play *coinchée*."

"So he played *coinchée* with his friends. He lived with his mother, didn't he? A good woman, unless I'm mistaken."

"Hmm!"

"What did you say?"

"Nothing. You're the one who's doing all the talking and I don't know what you're getting at."

Upstairs, Inspector Cavre was getting dressed.

"Does she live far from here?"

"At the end of the street, in a small yard. It's the house with three stone steps."

"Do you happen to know if my friend Cavre—the man who's lodging here with you—has been to see her yet?"

"And how do you think he could have been to see her when he's only just getting up?"

"Is he staying here long?"

"I haven't asked him."

She opened the windows and pushed back the shutters. A milky-white light filtered into the room, for day had already broken.

"Do *you* think Retailleau was drunk that night?"

The woman suddenly became aggressive and snapped back:

"No more drunk than you are, drinking cognac at eight in the morning!"

"How much do I owe you?"

"Two francs."

The Trois Mules, a rather more modern-looking inn, was just opposite, but the superintendent did not think he would gain anything by going inside. A blacksmith was lighting the fire in his forge. A woman standing on her doorstep was throwing a bucket of dirty water into the street. A bell, the sound of which reminded Maigret of his childhood, tinkled lightly and a boy wearing clogs came out of the baker's with a loaf of bread under his arm.

Curtains parted as he made his way down the street. A hand wiped the condensation from a window and a wrinkled old face with eyes that were ringed with red like Inspector Cavre's peered through the windowpane. On the right stood the church. It was built of gray stone and covered with slates that looked black and shiny after the heavy rain. A very thin woman of about fifty, in deep mourning and holding herself very erect, came out of the church with a prayerbook covered in black cloth in her hand.

Maigret stood idly for a moment in a corner of the little square by a board marked "School" which had doubtless been put up to caution motorists. He followed the woman with his eyes. The moment he saw her disappear into a kind of blind alley at the end of the street, he guessed at once that it was Madame Retailleau. Since Cavre had not yet visited her, he quickened his step.

He had guessed right, for when he got to the corner of the alley, he saw the woman go up three steps to the door of a small house and take a key out of her bag. A few minutes later, he knocked at the glass door behind which hung a lace curtain.

"Come in."

She had just had time to take off her coat and her black crepe veil. The prayerbook was still on the oilcloth which covered the table. The white enamel kitchen stove was already lit. The top was so clean that it must have been painstakingly rubbed with sandpaper.

"Please forgive me for disturbing you, madame. It is Madame Retailleau, isn't it?"

He did not assert himself very forcefully, for neither her voice nor her movements gave him much encouragement. She stood quite still with her hands over her stomach, her face almost the color of wax, and waited for Maigret to speak.

"I have been asked to investigate the rumors that are circulating with regard to the death of your son . . ."

"Who are you?"

"Superintendent Maigret of the Police Judiciaire. Let me hasten to add that these inquiries are for the moment unofficial."

"What does that mean?"

"That the case has not yet been laid before the court."

"What case?"

"I am sorry to have to talk about such unpleasant matters, madame, but you are no doubt aware of the various rumors connected with your son's death . . ."

"You cannot stop people from talking . . ."

In order to gain time, Maigret had turned towards a photograph in an oval giltwood frame which was hanging on the wall to the left of the walnut kitchen dresser. It was an enlarged photograph of a man of about thirty with a crew cut and a large mustache drooping over his lips.

"Is that your husband?"

"Yes."

"Unless I'm mistaken, you had the misfortune to lose him unexpectedly when your son was still a small boy. From what I have been told, you were forced to bring an action against the dairy that employed him in order to receive a pension."

"You have not been told the truth. There was never any court case. Monsieur Oscar Drouhet, the manager of the dairy, did what was necessary."

"And later, when your son was old enough to work, he took him into the business. Your son was his book-keeper, I believe."

"He did the work of the assistant manager. He would have been made assistant manager if he hadn't been so young."

"You haven't got a photograph of him, have you?"

Maigret could have kicked himself, for as he spoke he saw a tiny photograph on a small round table covered with red plush. He picked it up quickly in case Madame Retailleau objected.

"How old was Albert when this photograph was taken?"

"Nineteen. It was taken last year."

He was a handsome boy with rather a wide face, greedy lips and merry, sparkling eyes. He looked healthy and strong.

Madame Retailleau stood waiting, as before, and let out an occasional sigh.

"He wasn't engaged?"

"No."

"As far as you know, he had no relationships with women?"

"My son was too young to be chasing women. He was a serious boy and only thought about his career."

This was not the impression the photograph gave. Young Albert Retailleau had the impassioned look of youth, thick glossy hair and a well-developed physique.

"What was your reaction when . . . I do apologize . . . You must see what I am getting at . . . Do you believe it was an accident?"

"One has to believe it was . . ."

"You had no suspicions whatsoever, then?"

"What sort of suspicions?"

"He never mentioned Mademoiselle Naud? . . . He never used to come home late at night?"

"No."

"And Monsieur Naud hasn't been to see you since your son died?"

"We have nothing to say to each other."

"I see . . . But he could have . . . Monsieur Groult-Cotelle hasn't called on you either, I take it?"

Was it Maigret's imagination, or had her eyes hardened momentarily? Maigret was sure they had.

"No," she murmured.

"So that you consider the rumors concerning the circumstances of your son's death to be quite untrue . . ."

"Yes, I do. I pay no attention to them. I don't want to know what people are saying. And if it's Monsieur Naud who sent you, you can go back and tell him what I've said."

For a few seconds, Maigret stood perfectly still, with his eyes half-shut and repeated to himself what she had said, as if to lodge it in his mind:

And if it's Monsieur Naud who sent you, you can go back and tell him what I've said.

Did she know that it was Etienne Naud who had greeted Maigret at the station the day before? Did she know that it was he, indirectly, who had caused him to make the journey from Paris? Or did she merely suspect this to be the case?

"Forgive me for having taken the liberty of calling on you, madame, especially at such an early hour."

"Time is of no importance to me."

"Goodbye, madame . . ."

She remained where she was and said not a word as Maigret walked toward the door and closed it behind him. The superintendent had not gone ten paces when he saw Inspector Cavre standing on the pavement as if he were on sentry duty.

Was Cavre waiting for Maigret to leave so that he, in turn, could talk to Albert's mother? Maigret wanted to find out once and for all. The conversation he had just had with Madame Retailleau had put him in a bad temper and he was in the mood to play a trick on his former colleague.

He relit his pipe, which he had put out with his thumb before entering Madame Retailleau's house, crossed the street and took up his position on the other side of the road, immediately opposite Cavre, standing resolutely on the pavement as if he meant to stay.

The town was awakening. Children were walking up to the school gate on one side of the little square in front of the church. Most of them had come from far afield and were muffled up in scarves and thick blue or red woolen socks. Many were wearing clogs.

"Well, old chap, it's your turn now! Off you go!" Maigret seemed to be saying, with a mischievous glint in his eyes.

Cavre did not move, but looked haughtily in the other direction as if he were above any such frivolities.

Had Madame Retailleau summoned him to Saint-Aubin? It was quite possible. She was a strange woman and it was very difficult to size her up. She had the characteristic, almost inborn mistrust of the peasant, while a certain disdain made her more like a well-to-do lady from the provinces. Beneath the cold exterior, one sensed an arrogance which nothing could undermine. The way she had stood motionless in front of Maigret was impressive in itself. She had not moved a step or made any kind of gesture while he had been in her house, but had stiffened as some animals are supposed to do when, confronted with danger, they feign death. She had only said a few words and her lips barely moved as she spoke.

"Well, Cavre, you old misery! Make up your mind . . .
Do something . . ."

Old Cadaver was stamping his feet to keep warm
but seemed in no hurry to make any sort of move as
long as Maigret was watching him.

It was a ridiculous situation. It was childish stub-
bornly to remain where he was, but Maigret did just
that. Unfortunately, however, this tactic turned out to
be a waste of time. At half past eight, a small, red-faced
man came out of his house and made his way to the
mairie. He opened the door with a key and a moment
afterwards Cavre followed him inside.

This was the very move that Maigret had intended
to make himself that morning, for he had determined to
find out what the local authorities had to say. His former colleague had beaten him to it and there was nothing for it but to wait his turn.

3

AN UNDESIRABLE PERSON

Henceforth, Maigret refused to discuss this undignified episode. He never spoke of what happened that day, and particularly that morning, and no doubt he would have preferred to forget the occasion.

The most disconcerting thing of all was losing the feeling that he *was* Maigret. For what, in fact, did he represent in Saint-Aubin? The short answer was nothing. Justin Cavre had gone into the *mairie* to talk to the local authorities while he, Maigret, had stood awkwardly outside in the street. The row of houses looked like a line of large, poisonous mushrooms clustered as they were beneath a sky that reminded one of a blister ready to burst. Maigret knew he was being watched for faces were peering at him from behind every curtain.

Admittedly, he did not really mind what a few old ladies or the butcher's wife thought. People could take him for what they liked and laugh at him as he went by, as some children had done as they went through the school gate, for all he cared.

It was just that he felt he was not the Maigret he was accustomed to be. Although perhaps it was an exaggeration to say he was thoroughly out of sorts, the simple fact of the matter was that he just did not feel himself.

What would happen, for example, if he were to go into the white-washed *mairie* and knock at the gray door on which "Secretary's Office" was written in black letters? He would be asked to wait his turn, just as if he had come in to see about a birth certificate or a claim of some sort. And meanwhile, old Cadaver would continue questioning the secretary in his tiny overheated office for as long as he liked.

Maigret was not here in an official capacity. He could not say he was acting on behalf of the Police Judiciaire, and in any case, who was to know whether anyone in this village surrounded by slimy marshland and stagnant water had even heard the name Maigret?

He was to find out soon enough. As he was waiting impatiently for Cavre to come out, he had one of the most extraordinary ideas in his entire career. He was all set to pursue relentlessly his former colleague, even to follow him step by step and say point-blank:

"Look here, Cavre, there's no point in trying to outwit each other. It is quite obvious you're not here for the fun of it. Someone asked you to come. Just tell me who it is and what you've been asked to do . . ."

How comparatively simple a proper, official investigation seemed at this moment! If he had been on a case somewhere within his own jurisdiction he would only have had to go into the local post office and say:

"Superintendent Maigret. Get me the Police Judiciaire as quickly as you can . . . Hello! Is that you, Janvier? . . . Jump in your car and come down here . . . When you see old Cadaver come out . . . Yes, Justin Cavre . . . Right . . . Follow him and don't let him out of your sight . . ."

Who knows? Maybe he would have had Etienne Naud tailed too, for he had just seen him drive past on the road to Fontenay.

Playing the role of Maigret was easy! An organization which ran like clockwork was at his disposal, besides which, he had only to say his name and people were so bowled over with admiration that they would do anything to please him.

But here, he was so little known that despite numerous articles and photographs which were always appearing in the newspapers, someone like Etienne Naud had walked straight up to Justin Cavre at the station.

Naud had looked after him well because his brother-in-law, the examining magistrate, had sent him all the way from Paris, but on the other hand, had they not all looked as if they were wondering what in fact he had come for? The gist of what their welcome meant was this:

"My brother-in-law Bréjon is a charming fellow who wants to help, but he has been away from Saint-Aubin far too long and has got quite the wrong idea of the situation. It was kind of him to have thought of sending you here. It is kind of you to have come. We will look after you as best we can. Eat and drink your fill. Let me show you around the estate. Don't, on any account, feel you have to stay in this damp, unattractive part of the world. And don't feel you have to look into this trivial matter which concerns no one but ourselves."

On whose behalf was he working, in fact? For Etienne Naud. But it was palpably obvious that Etienne Naud did not want him to carry out a proper investigation.

And to cap it all, Geneviève had come into his room in the middle of the night and had admitted:

"I was Albert Retailleau's mistress and I am pregnant by him. But I'll kill myself if you breathe a word to my parents."

Now, if she really was Albert's mistress, the accusations against Naud suddenly took on a terrible meaning. Had she thought of that? Had she consciously charged her father with murder?

And even the victim's mother, who had said nothing, admitted nothing, denied nothing, had made it perfectly clear by her attitude that she did not want Maigret interfering. It was none of his business was what she implied.

Everyone, even the old ladies lying in wait behind their fluttering curtains, even the schoolchildren who had turned around to stare as they went by, considered him an intruder, an undesirable person. Worse still, no one knew where this steady plodder had come from or why he was in this village.

And so, in a setting which was exactly right for the part, with hands sunk into the pockets of his heavy overcoat, Maigret looked just like one of those nasty characters tormented by some secret vice who prowl round the Porte Saint-Martin or somewhere similar with hunched shoulders and sidelong glances and cautiously edge their way past the houses well out of sight of the police.

Was he turning into another Cavre? He felt like sending someone to Naud's house to fetch his suitcase and taking the first train back to Paris. He would tell Bréjon:

"They won't have anything to do with me . . . Leave your brother-in-law to his own devices . . ."

All the same, he had gone into the *mairie* as soon as the ex-inspector emerged with a leather briefcase tucked under his arm. No doubt this would increase his standing in the village, for now he would pass for a lawyer.

The secretary was a little man who smelt rather unpleasant. He did not get up as Maigret entered his office.

"Can I help you?"

"Superintendent Maigret of the Police Judiciaire. I am in Saint-Aubin on unofficial business and I would like to ask you one or two questions."

The little man hesitated and looked annoyed, but

nonetheless invited Maigret to sit down on a wicker-seated chair.

"Did the private detective who has just left your office tell you whom he was working for?"

The secretary either did not understand or pretended he did not understand the question. And he reacted in similar fashion to all the other questions the superintendent put to him.

"You knew Albert Retailleau. Tell me what you thought of him."

"He was a good sort . . . Yes, that's how I'd describe him, a good sort . . . You couldn't fault him . . ."

"Did he like to chase women?"

"He was only a lad, you know, and we don't always know what the young are up to, these days, but you couldn't say he ran after women . . ."

"Was he Mademoiselle Naud's lover?"

"People said he was . . . Rumors were going around . . . But it's all pure hearsay . . ."

"Who discovered the body?"

"Ferchaud, the station master. He telephoned the *mairie* and the deputy mayor immediately contacted the Benet gendarmerie as there isn't a constabulary in Saint-Aubin."

"What did the doctor who examined the body say?"

"What did he say? Just that he was dead . . . There wasn't much of him left . . . The train went right over him . . ."

"But he was identified as Albert Retailleau?"

"What? . . . Of course . . . It was Retailleau all right, there was no doubt about that . . ."

"When did the last train pass through?"

"At 5:07 in the morning."

"Didn't people think it odd that Retailleau should have been on the railway line at five in the morning in the middle of winter?"

The secretary's reply was quite something:

"It was dry at the time. There was hoar frost on the ground."

"But people talked all the same . . ."

"Rumors circulated, yes . . . But you can never stop people from talking . . ."

"Your opinion then, is that Retailleau died a natural death?"

"It is very hard to say what happened."

And did Maigret bring up the subject of Madame Retailleau? He did, and the reply was as follows:

"She's a truly good woman. I can't say more."

And Naud, too, was described in similar terms:

"Such a likeable fellow. His father was a splendid person as well, a county councillor . . ."

And lastly, what did the secretary have to say about Geneviève?

"An attractive girl . . ."

"Well-behaved?"

"Of course she is well-behaved . . . And her mother is one of the most respected members of the community . . ."

The little man spoke politely enough, but his replies simply did not sound convincing. To make matters worse, he kept poking his finger up his nose as he spoke and would then carefully examine what he had picked out.

"And what is your opinion of Monsieur Groult-Cotelle?"

"He's a decent sort, too. A modest man . . ."

"Is he a close friend of the Nauds?"

"They see a good deal of one another, certainly. But that's only natural since they move in the same circles."

"When exactly was Retailleau's cap discovered not far from the Nauds' house?"

"When? . . . Well . . . But was it just the cap that was found?"

"I was told that someone called Désiré who collects the milk for the dairy found the cap in the reeds along the bank of the canal."

"So people said . . ."

"It's not true, then?"

"It's difficult to say. Désiré is drunk half the time."

"And when he is drunk . . ."

"Sometimes he tells the truth and sometimes he doesn't . . ."

"But a cap is something you can see and touch! Some people have seen it . . ."

"Ah!"

"It must have been put into safe-keeping by now . . ."

"Maybe . . . I don't know . . . May I remind you that this office is not a police station and we believe in minding our own business . . ."

This unpleasant-smelling, silly individual could not have spoken more plainly and was obviously delighted he had given a Parisian such short shrift.

A few moments later, Maigret was back in the street, no further on with his investigation than he had been before, but by now convinced that no one was going to help him find out the truth.

And since no one wanted to know the truth, what was the point of his being here? Would it not be more sensible to go back to Paris and say to Bréjon:

"Look . . . Your brother-in-law doesn't want there to be a proper investigation into all this . . . No one down there likes the idea . . . I have come back . . . They gave a wonderful dinner for me . . ."

Maigret passed a large house built of gray stone and saw from the bright yellow plaque on the wall that it belonged to the notary. This, then, was the house that Bréjon's father and sister had once occupied and in the gray, watery light it had the same air of timelessness and inscrutability as the rest of the town.

He walked a little further on until he came to the Lion d'Or. Inside, he could see someone talking to the woman who ran the inn and he had the distinct impression that they were talking about him and standing by the window in order to get a better view.

A man on a bicycle came into sight. Maigret recognized the rider as he approached but did not have time to turn away. Alban Groult-Cotelle was on his way home from the Nauds' and he jumped off his bicycle as soon as he saw Maigret.

"It's good to see you again . . . We're only a stone's throw away from my house . . . Will you do me the honor of coming in for a drink? . . . I insist! . . . My house is very modest but I've a few bottles of vintage port . . ."

Maigret followed him. He did not expect much to come of the visit but the prospect was infinitely preferable to wandering alone through the hostile town.

It was a huge, solid house which looked very appealing from a distance. Its squat shape, black railings and high slate roof gave it the air of a bourgeois fortress.

Inside, everything looked shabby and neglected. The surly-faced maid looked a real slut and yet it was obvious to Maigret from certain looks they gave each other that Groult-Cotelle was sleeping with her.

"I am sorry everything is so untidy . . . I'm a bachelor and live alone . . . I'm only interested in books, so . . ."

So . . . the wallpaper was peeling off the walls which were covered in damp patches, the curtains were gray with dust, and one had to try three or four chairs before finding one that did not wobble. Only one room on the first floor was heated, no doubt to save wood, and this served as a sitting room, dining room and library. There was even a divan in one corner which Maigret suspected his host slept on most of the time.

"Do sit down . . . It really is a pity you didn't come in the summer as it is rather more attractive round here then . . . How do you like my friends the Nauds? . . . What a nice family they are! I know them well . . . You would not find a better man than Naud anywhere . . . He may not be a very deep thinker, he may be a tiny bit arrogant, but he is so unaffected and sincere . . . He is very rich, you know."

"And Geneviève Naud?"

"A charming girl . . . Without any . . . Yes, charming is how I'd describe her . . ."

"I presume I'll have the opportunity to meet her . . . She'll soon be better, I hope?"

"Of course she will . . . of course . . . She's just like any other young girl of her age . . . Cheers . . ."

"Did you know Retailleau?"

"By sight . . . His mother seems to be well thought of . . . I would show you around if you were here for longer as there are some interesting people scattered here and there in the villages roundabout . . . My uncle, the general, frequently used to say that it is in country districts and especially here in La Vendée that . . ."

Pure waffle! If Maigret gave Groult-Cotelle the chance he would start telling him the history of every family in the neighborhood all over again.

"I am afraid I must go now . . ."

"Oh yes! Your investigations! . . . How are you getting on? Are you optimistic? . . . If you want my opinion, the answer is to get hold of whoever is responsible for all these false rumors . . ."

"Have you any idea who it might be?"

"Me? Of course not. Don't start thinking I have any bright ideas on the subject, please . . . I'll probably see you this evening, as Etienne has asked me to dinner and unless I'm too busy . . ."

Busy doing what, pray? Anyone would think that words in this particular neighborhood took on a completely different meaning.

"Have you heard the rumor about the cap?"

"What cap? Oh, yes . . . I was lost for a moment . . . I did hear some vague story . . . But is it true? Has it really been found? That's the key to it all, isn't it?"

No, that was not the key to it all. The young girl's confession, for example, was just as important as the discovery of the cap. But would Maigret be able to keep to himself what he knew much longer?

Five minutes later, Maigret rang the doctor's bell. A little maid answered the door and started to explain that the surgery was closed until one o'clock. He must have persisted for he was shown into the garage where a tall, strapping fellow with a cheerful face was repairing a motorbike.

It was the same old story:

"Superintendent Maigret of the Police Judiciaire . . . I'm here in an unofficial capacity . . ."

"I'll show you into my office, if I may, and then when I've washed my hands . . ."

Maigret waited near the folding table which was used to examine the patients. It was covered with an oilcloth.

"So you're the famous Superintendent Maigret? I've heard quite a lot about you . . . I've a friend who pores over the miscellaneous news items in the papers . . . He lives thirty-five kilometers away, but if he knew you were in Saint-Aubin he'd be over here like a shot . . . You solved the Landru case, didn't you?"

He had hit on one of the very few cases Maigret had had nothing to do with.

"And to what do we owe the honor of your presence in Saint-Aubin? For it is, indeed, an honor . . . I am sure you would like something to drink . . . I'm looking after a sick child at the moment and I've left him in the sitting room as it's warmer there, so I have had to bring you in here . . . Will you have a brandy?"

And that was all. Maigret just drank his brandy.

"Retailleau? A charming boy . . . I believe he was a good son to his mother . . . She never complained about him, at any rate . . . She's one of my patients . . . a strange woman whom life ought to have treated better. She came from a good family, too. Everyone was amazed when she married Joseph Retailleau, a commoner who worked in the dairy.

"Etienne Naud? He's a real character ... We go shooting together ... He's a crack shot ... Groult-Cotelle? No, you could hardly call him a good shot, but that's because he is very short-sighted ...

"So, you have met everyone already ... Have you seen Tine, too? ... You haven't seen Tine yet? ... Note that I mention her name with great respect, like everyone else in Saint-Aubin ... Tine is Madame Naud's mother ... Madame Bréjon, if you prefer ... Her son is an examining magistrate in Paris ... Yes, that's right ... he's the one you must know ... His mother was a La Noue, one of the great families in La Vendée ... She does not want to be a bother to her daughter and son-in-law and she lives alone, near the church ... at the age of eighty-two, she's still sound of wind and limb and she's one of my worst patients ...

"You're staying in Saint-Aubin for a few days, are you?

"What? The cap? Oh, yes ... No, I haven't heard anything about that myself ... Well, I did hear one or two rumors ...

"All this was discovered rather late in the day, you see ... If I had known at the time, I would have carried out an autopsy ... But put yourself in my position ... I was told the poor boy had been run over by a train ... It was patently obvious to me he *had* been run over by a train and naturally, I wrote my report along those lines ..."

Maigret scowled, for he could have sworn that they

were all in league with one another, that whether peevish or merry like the doctor, they had passed around
the story as they might pass around a ball, giving each
other knowing looks as they did so.

The sky was almost bright, now. Reflections shone
in all the puddles and patches of mud glistened in
places.

The superintendent walked up the main street once
more. He had not looked to see what it was called but
it was most probably the Rue de la République. He
decided to go into the Trois Mules, opposite the Lion
d'Or, where he had received such a cold welcome that
morning.

The bar was brighter than that of the Lion d'Or,
with framed prints and a photograph of a president
who had held office some thirty or forty years earlier
hanging on the whitewashed walls. Behind the bar was
another room, deserted and gloomy-looking; this was
evidently where the locals came to dance on Sundays,
for there was a platform at one end and the room was
festooned with paper chains.

Four men were seated at a table, enjoying a bottle
of full-bodied wine. One of them coughed affectedly
when the superintendent came in, as if to say to the
others:

"There he is . . ."

Maigret sat down on one of the benches at the other
end of the table. This time, he felt the atmosphere was

different, for the men had stopped talking and he knew full well that before he came in, they would certainly not have been drinking and looking at each other in silence as they sat at the table.

They looked just like characters in a dumb show as they sat together in a huddle, their elbows and shoulders touching. Eventually, the oldest of the four men, a plowman by the look of the whip beside him, spat on the floor, whereupon the others burst out laughing.

Was that long stream of spittle meant for Maigret?

"What can I get you?" inquired a young woman, tilting her hips in order to hold her grubby-looking baby.

"I'd like some of your *vin rosé*."

"A jug?"

"All right . . ."

Maigret puffed furiously at his pipe. Up until now the townsfolk had concealed or at any rate disguised their hostility towards him, but now they were sneering at him, indeed, deliberately provoking him.

"Even the dirtiest jobs have got to be done, if you ask me, sonny boy," said the plowman after a long silence, no one having asked him for his opinion in the first place.

His cronies roared with laughter at this, as if that simple pronouncement had some extraordinary significance for them. One man, however, did not laugh, a young lad of eighteen or nineteen with pale gray eyes and a pock-marked face. Leaning on one elbow, he looked Maigret straight in the eye, as if he wanted him to feel the full force of his hatred or contempt.

"Some people have no pride!" growled another man.

"If you've got the cash, pride doesn't often come into it . . ."

Perhaps their remarks did not amount to anything very much, but Maigret got the message, nonetheless. He had finally clashed with the opposition party, to describe the situation in political terms.

Who could know for sure? Undoubtedly, all the rumors flying about had originated in the Trois Mules. And if the townspeople laid the blame at Maigret's door, they obviously thought Etienne Naud was paying him to hush up the truth.

"Tell me, gentlemen . . ."

Maigret rose to his feet and walked towards them. Although not timid by nature, he felt the blood rushing to his ears.

He was greeted in total silence. Only the young boy went on glowering at the superintendent, while the others, looking rather awkward, turned their heads away.

"Those of you who live around here may be able to help me in the course of justice."

They were suspicious, the rascals. Maigret's words had certainly stirred them up, but they still would not give in. The old man muttered crossly, looking at his spittle on the floor:

"Justice for who? For Naud?"

The superintendent ignored the remark and went on talking. Meanwhile, the *patronne* hovered in the kitchen doorway, standing there with the child in her arms.

"In order for justice to be carried out, I need to discover two things in particular. Firstly, I need to find one of Retailleau's friends, a real friend and if possible someone who was with him on that last evening . . ."

Maigret realized that the person in question was the youngest of the four men, for the other three glanced in his direction.

"Secondly, I need to find the cap. You know what I'm talking about."

"Go on, Louis!" growled the plowman, as he rolled a cigarette. But the young man was still not convinced.

"Who's sent you?"

It was certainly the first time Maigret's authority had been questioned by a young country lad. And yet it was essential that he explained himself, for he was determined to gain the lad's confidence.

"Superintendent Maigret, Police Judiciaire . . ."

Who knows? Perhaps luck would have it that the boy had heard of him. But alas, this was not the case.

"Why are you staying with the Nauds?"

"Because he was told I was coming and was at the station to meet me. And as I didn't know the neighborhood . . ."

"There are inns . . ."

"I didn't know that when I arrived . . ."

"Who's the man in the inn across the road?"

It was Maigret who was being interrogated!

"A private detective . . ."

"Who's he working for?"

"I don't know."

"Why is there still no proper inquiry into the affair? Albert died three weeks ago . . ."

"That's the stuff, my boy! Go on!" the three men seemed to be saying to the youngster, rigid in front of them with a grim look on his face in an effort to combat his shyness.

"No one lodged a complaint."

"So you can kill anyone, and so long as no one lodges a complaint . . ."

"The doctor concluded it was an accident."

"Was he there when it happened?"

"As soon as I have enough evidence, the inquiry will be made official . . ."

"What do you mean by evidence?"

"Well, if we could prove that the cap was discovered between Naud's house and the place where the body was found, for example . . ."

"We'll have to take him to Désiré," said the stoutest of the men, who was wearing a carpenter's overall. "Give us another one, Mélie . . . Bring us another glass . . ."

Even now, it was a victory for Maigret.

"What time did Retailleau leave the café that night?"

"About half past eleven . . ."

"Were there many people in the café?"

"Four . . . We played *coinchée* . . ."

"Did you all leave together?"

"The two other men took the road to the left . . . I went part of the way with Albert."

"In which direction?"

"Towards Naud's house."

"Did Albert confide in you?"

"No."

The young lad's face darkened. He said no reluctantly, for he obviously wanted to be scrupulously honest.

"He didn't say why he was going to the Nauds'?"

"No. He was very angry."

"Who with?"

"With her."

"You mean Mademoiselle Naud? Had he told you about her before?"

"Yes . . ."

"What did he tell you?"

"Everything and nothing . . . Not in words . . . He used to go there nearly every night . . ."

"Did he brag about it?"

"No." He gave Maigret a look of reproach. "He was in love and everyone could see he was. He couldn't hide it."

"And he was angry with her on that last day?"

"Yes. Something was on his mind the whole evening, for he kept on looking at his watch as we played cards. Just as we parted company on the road . . ."

"Where exactly?"

"Five hundred yards from the Nauds' house . . ."

"The place, then, where he was found dead?"

"More or less . . . I had gone half way with him . . ."

"And you are sure he went on along the road?"

"Yes . . . He squeezed my hands and said with tears in his eyes: 'It's all over, Louis, old chap. . .' "

"What was all over?"

"It was all over between him and Geneviève . . . That's what I assumed . . . He meant he was going to see her for the last time."

"But did he go?"

"There was a moon that night . . . It was freezing . . . I could still see him when he was only about a hundred yards from the house."

"And the cap?"

Young Louis got up and looked at the others, his mind made up.

"Come with me . . ."

"Can you trust him, Louis?" asked one of the older men. "Be careful, son."

But Louis was at the age when one is prepared to risk all to win all. He looked Maigret in the eye as if to say: "You're a real blackguard if you let me down!"

"Follow me . . . I live very near here . . ."

"Your glass . . . Yours, superintendent . . . And you

can believe everything the lad says, I promise . . . He's as honest as they come, that boy . . ."

"Your good health, gentlemen . . ."

Maigret had no choice but to drink a toast with the four men. The large glasses made a tinkling sound as they clinked them together. He then followed Louis out of the room, completely forgetting to pay for his jug of wine.

As they came outside, Maigret saw old Cadaver on the opposite side of the road. He had his briefcase under his arm and was about to go into the Lion d'Or. Was Maigret mistaken? It seemed to him that his former colleague had a sardonic smile on his face, although he only caught a glimpse of him sideways on.

"Come with me . . . This way . . ."

They made their way along narrow lanes which were quite unknown to Maigret and which linked up with the three or four streets in the village. They came to a row of cottages, each with its own tiny fenced-in front garden. Louis pushed open a small gate with a bell attached to it and called out:

"It's me!"

He went into a kitchen where four or five children were sitting round the table having their lunch.

"What is it, Louis?" asked his mother, looking uncomfortably at Maigret.

"Wait here . . . I'll be back in a minute, monsieur . . ."

Louis rushed up the stairs which led down to the kitchen itself and went into a room. Maigret heard the sound of a drawer being pulled open, of someone walking about and knocking over a chair. Downstairs, meanwhile, Louis's mother shut the kitchen door but did not really know whether or not to make Maigret welcome.

Louis came downstairs, pale and worried-looking.

"Someone's stolen it!" he declared, with a stony expression on his face.

And then, turning to his mother, he said in a harsh voice:

"Someone's been here . . . Who was it? . . . Who came here this morning?"

"Look, Louis . . ."

"Who? Tell me who it was! Who stole the cap?"

"I don't even know what cap you're talking about . . ."

"Someone went up to my room . . ."

He was in such an excited state that he looked as if he was about to hit his mother.

"Will you please calm down! Can't you see how rude you're being, speaking to me in that tone of voice?"

"Have you been in the house all morning?"

"I went out to the butcher's and the baker's . . ."

"And what about the little ones?"

"I took the two youngest boys next door, as usual. The two that are not yet at school."

"Forgive me, superintendent. I just don't understand. The cap was in my drawer this morning. I am positive it was. I saw it . . ."

"But what cap do you mean? Will you answer me

that? Anyone would think you've taken leave of your senses! You'd do better to sit down and have your lunch . . . As for this gentleman you've left standing . . ."

But Louis gave his mother a pointed look, full of suspicion, and pulled Maigret outside.

"Come with me . . . I have something else to say . . . I swear, over my father's dead body, that the cap . . ."

THE THEFT OF THE CAP

The impatient youngster walked quickly up the street, his neck taut and his body bent forward as he pulled the reluctant Maigret along with him. Here he was, being guided almost by force towards unknown delights by a glib and persuasive younger man, and the situation made him extremely uneasy. Such equivocal circumstances reminded him of a common enough scene in Montmartre, where one would see the doormen of dubious-looking clubs push an intimidated gentleman through the doors, against his will.

Louis's mother stood on the doorstep and shouted as they were going round the corner of the little street:

"Aren't you going to have your lunch, Louis?"

Was Maigret the only one who heard? He was spurred on by strong feelings. He had promised this gentleman from Paris he would do something and now he was unable to keep his word because an unexpected occurrence had complicated matters. Would he not be taken for an impostor? Was he not endangering the cause he had all too hastily championed?

"I want Désiré to tell you himself. The cap was in my bedroom. I wonder if my mother was telling the truth."

Maigret was wondering the same thing and at the same time thought of Inspector Cavre, whom he could picture vividly wheedling information out of the woman with six children.

"What time is it?"

"Ten past twelve."

"Désiré will still be at the dairy. Let's go this way. It's quicker."

Again, Louis led Maigret through little alleyways, past small, shabby houses which the superintendent had never seen before; once, a sow covered in mud rushed at their legs.

"One evening, the evening of the funeral, in fact, old Désiré came into the Lion d'Or and threw a cap on the table. Speaking in patois, he asked whose it was. I recognized it straightaway as I was with Albert when he bought it in Niort. I remembered having a discussion with him about what color he should get."

"What is your trade?" asked Maigret.

"I'm a carpenter. The largest of the men you saw just now in the Trois Mules is my boss. Well, Désiré was drunk that evening. There were at least six people in the café. I asked him where he found the cap. Désiré collects the milk from the little farms in the marshland, you see, and as you can't get to them by road in a truck, he does his rounds by boat . . .

"'I found it in the reeds,' he said, 'very near the dead poplar.'

"I repeat, there were at least six people who heard him say this. Everyone here knows that the dead poplar is between the Nauds' house and the spot where Albert's body was found . . .

"This way . . . We're going to the dairy. You can see the chimney stack over there, on the left."

They had left the village behind them. Dark hedges enclosed tiny gardens. A little further on, the dairy came into view. The low buildings were painted white and the tall chimney stack stood straight up against the sky.

"I don't know why I decided to shove the cap into my pocket . . . I already had the feeling that too many people were keen to hush up this whole affair . . .

"'It's young Retailleau's cap,' someone said.

"And Désiré, drunk as he was, frowned, for he suddenly realized that he was not supposed to have found it where he did.

"'Désiré, are you sure it was near the dead poplar?'

"Well, superintendent, the very next day, he didn't want to admit to anything. When he was asked exactly where he had found it, he would say:

"'Over there . . . I don't really know exactly! Just leave me alone, will you! I'm sick of this cap business . . .'"

Flat-bottomed boats filled with pitchers of milk were tied up beside the dairy.

"I say, Philippe . . . Has old Désiré gone home?"

"He can't have gone home, seeing as he never set out . . . He must have got plastered yesterday as he didn't do his round this morning."

An idea flashed through Maigret's mind.

"Would the manager be around at this time of day, do you think?" he asked his companion.

"He'll probably be in his office . . . The little door at the side . . ."

"Wait here a minute . . ."

Oscar Drouhet, the manager of the dairy, was in fact on the telephone when Maigret walked in. The superintendent introduced himself. Drouhet had the serious, steadfast manner of any local craftsman turned small businessman. Pulling on his pipe with short, sharp puffs, he observed Maigret and let him speak, trying all the while to size him up.

"Albert Retailleau's father was once in your employment, I believe? I've been told he was the victim of an accident at the dairy . . ."

"One of the boilers exploded."

"I understand his widow receives a considerable income from you?"

He was an intelligent man, for he realized immediately that Maigret's question was loaded with innuendoes.

"What do you mean?"

"Did his widow take you to court, or did you yourself . . ."

"Don't try to complicate the issue. It was my fault the accident happened. Retailleau had been saying for at least two months that the boiler needed a complete overhaul and even that it should be replaced. It was the busiest time of the year and I kept putting it off."

"Were your workmen insured?"

"Nowhere near adequately . . ."

"Forgive me. Let me ask you whether you were the one who didn't think they were adequately insured, or if . . ."

Once more, they both understood each other perfectly, and Maigret did not have to finish his sentence.

"His widow lodged a complaint against us, as she was entitled to do," Oscar Drouhet admitted.

"I am sure," the superintendent went on, smiling slightly, "she did not approach you merely to ask you to go into the question of compensation pay. She sent lawyers to investigate . . ."

"Is that so unusual? A woman knows nothing of these things, would you not agree? I acknowledged the validity of her claim and in addition to the pension she received from the insurance company, I elected to give her a further sum which I pay out of my own pocket. On top of this, I paid for her son's education and took him on here as soon as he was old enough to work. My kindness was rewarded, what's more, for he was a hard-working, honest lad. Albert was a clever boy and quite capable of running the dairy in my absence . . ."

"Thank you . . . Or rather, just one more question:

Albert's mother hasn't called on you since the death of her son, has she?"

Drouhet managed not to smile, but his brown eyes flickered briefly.

"No," he said, "she hasn't come to see me *yet*."

Maigret had been right, then, in this respect. Madame Retailleau was indeed a woman who knew how to defend herself and attack, if need be. She was undoubtedly the sort of person who would never lose sight of her interests.

"It seems that Désiré, your milk collector, did not come to work this morning?"

"That often happens . . . On the days he is more drunk than usual . . ."

Maigret went back to the pock-marked youth, who was terrified he would no longer be taken seriously.

"What did he say? He's a good sort, but he's really on the other side . . ."

"Whose side?"

"Monsieur Naud's, the doctor's, the mayor's . . . He couldn't have said anything against me . . ."

"Of course not . . ."

"We've got to find old Désiré . . . We could go around to his house, if you like . . . It's not far . . ."

They set off again, both forgetting it was lunchtime, and eventually came to a house on the fringe of the little town. Louis knocked on a glass door, pushed it open and shouted into the semi-darkness:

"Désiré! Hey! Désiré!"

But only a cat emerged and rubbed itself against the boy's legs. Meanwhile, Maigret came upon a kind of den which consisted of a bed without a cover or a pillow where Désiré obviously slept with all his clothes on, a small, cracked iron stove, a bundle of rags, empty bottles and old bones.

"He must have gone off drinking somewhere. Come on . . ."

Still the same concern he would not be taken seriously.

"He worked on Etienne Naud's farm, you see . . . He's still on good terms with them, even though he was sacked. He's the sort of person who wants to be on good terms with everyone, and that is why he put on an act when people started asking him questions about the cap the day after he found it.

"'What cap? Ah, yes! The tattered one I picked up somewhere or other, I've forgotten where . . . I've no idea what's happened to it . . .'

"Well, monsieur, I for one can tell you that there were blood stains on the cap. And I wrote and told the Director of Prosecutions . . ."

"So it was you who wrote the anonymous letters?"

"I wrote three, so if there were more, someone else must have written them. I wrote about the cap and then about Albert's relationship with Geneviève Naud . . . Wait, perhaps Désiré is in here . . ."

Louis had darted into a grocer's shop, but through the windows Maigret could see there were bottles at the

end of the counter and two tables at the back of the
shop for customers' use. The youngster looked crest-
fallen as he came out again.

"He was here early this morning. He must have done
the rounds . . ."

Maigret had only been into two cafés: the Lion d'Or
and the Trois Mules. In less than half an hour, he came
to know a dozen or more, not cafés in the true sense of
the word, but premises the average passer-by would not
have suspected were licensed. The harnessmaker had a
kind of bar next to his workshop and the farrier had a
similar arrangement. Old Désiré had been seen in almost every bar they visited.

"How was he?"

"He was well enough."

And they knew what that meant.

"He was in a hurry when he left, as he had to go to
the post office . . ."

"The post office is shut," Louis said. "But I know
the postmistress, and she'll open up if I tap on her
window."

"Especially when she knows I've a call to make,"
said Maigret.

And sure enough, as soon as the boy tapped on the
pane, the window opened.

"Is that you, Louis? What do you want?"

"It's the gentleman from Paris. He wants to make a
call."

"I'll open up right away . . ."

Maigret asked to be put through to the Nauds.

"Hello! Who is it speaking?"

He did not recognize the voice, a man's voice.

"Hello! Who did you say? Ah! Forgive me . . . Alban, yes . . . I hadn't realized . . . Maigret, here . . . Could you tell Madame Naud I shan't be coming back for lunch? Give her my apologies. No, it's nothing important . . . I don't know when I'll be back . . ."

As he left the booth, he saw from the look on his young companion's face that he had something interesting to tell him.

"How much do I owe you, mademoiselle? . . . Thank you . . . I'm sorry to have bothered you."

Back in the street once more, Louis informed Maigret excitedly:

"I *told* you something was afoot. Old Désiré came in on the dot of eleven. Do you know what he posted? He sent a money order for five hundred francs to his son in Morocco . . . His son's up to no good. He left home without any warning. He and his father used to quarrel and fight every day . . . Désiré's never been known to be anything other than drunk, as it were . . . And now his son writes to him from time to time, either complaining or asking for money . . . But all his money goes on drink, you see . . . The old man never has a sou . . . Sometimes he sends a money order for ten or twenty francs at the beginning of the month . . . I wonder . . .

Wait a minute . . . If you still have time, we'll go and see his stepsister . . ."

The streets, the houses they had been walking past all morning, were now becoming familiar to the superintendent. He was beginning to recognize people's faces and the names painted above the shops. Rather than brighten up, the sky had clouded over again and the air was heavy with moisture. Soon there would be fog.

"His stepsister knits for a living. She's an old spinster and used to work for our last priest. This is her house . . ."

He went up three steps to the blue-painted front door, knocked and then opened it.

"Désiré's not here, is he?"

He then beckoned Maigret to come inside.

"Hello, Désiré . . . I'm sorry to barge in like this, Mademoiselle Jeanne . . . There's a gentleman from Paris who'd like to have a few words with your stepbrother . . ."

The tiny room was very clean. The table stood near a mahogany bed covered with an enormous red eiderdown. Maigret glanced round and saw a crucifix with a sprig of boxwood behind it, a figure of the Virgin Mary in a glass case on the chest of drawers, and two cutlets on a plate with writing round the picture on it.

Désiré tried to stand up but knew he was in danger of falling off his chair. He maintained a dignified pose and muttering thickly, his tongue not being able to articulate the words, he said:

"What can I do for you?"

For he was polite. He was always anxious to make that clear.

"I may have drunk too much . . . Yes, maybe I've had a good few drinks, but I *am* polite, monsieur . . . Everyone'll tell you that Désiré is polite to one and all . . ."

"Look, Désiré, the gentleman wants to know exactly where you found the cap . . . You know, Albert's cap . . ."

These few words were enough. The drunkard's face hardened and assumed a totally blank expression. His watery eyes became even more glaucous.

"Don't play the fool, Désiré . . . I've got the cap . . . You remember, when you threw it on the table at François's place, that evening, and said you'd found it by the dead poplar . . ."

The old monkey was not satisfied with a simple denial. He smirked with delight and went on with more gusto than was necessary:

"Do you understand what he's saying, m'sieur? Why should I have thrown a cap on the table, I'd like to know? I've never worn a cap . . . Jeanne! Where's my hat? Show this gentleman my hat . . . These youngsters have no respect for their elders . . ."

"Désiré . . ."

"Désiré, indeed? . . . Désiré may be drunk, but he's polite and would be obliged if you'd call him Monsieur Désiré . . . Do you hear, you troublemaker, you bastard!"

"Have you heard from your son recently?" interrupted Maigret suddenly.

"So, it's my son, now, eh? You want to know what my son's been up to? Well, just let me tell you, he's a soldier! He's a brave fellow, my son!"

"That's what I thought. He'll certainly be pleased with the money order."

"Soon I won't be allowed to send my son a money order, is that it? Hey, Jeanne! Do you hear? And maybe I won't be allowed to come and have a bite to eat with my stepsister either!"

At the beginning, he had probably been frightened, but now he was really enjoying himself. He made himself a laughing-stock in the end, and when Maigret got up to go he followed him out to the front doorstep, staggering all the way, and would have followed him into the street if Jeanne had not stopped him.

"Désiré's polite . . . Do you hear, you rascal? And if anyone tells you, Monsieur Parisian, that Désiré's son is not a fine fellow . . ."

Doors opened. Maigret wanted to get away.

With tears in his eyes and his teeth clenched, Louis said emphatically:

"I swear to you, superintendent . . ."

"It's all right, lad, I believe you . . ."

"It's that man staying at the Lion d'Or, isn't it?"

"I think so. I'd like to have proof, though. Do you know anyone who was at the Lion d'Or last night?"

"I'm sure Liboureau's son was there. He goes in every evening."

"Right! I'll wait at the Trois Mules while you go

and ask him if he saw Désiré. Find out if the old man got into conversation with our visitor from Paris . . . Wait . . . We can eat at the Trois Mules, can't we? We'll have a bite of something together . . . Off you go, be quick . . ."

There was no tablecloth. The table was set with metal knives and forks. All that was offered at midday was a beetroot salad, rabbit and a piece of cheese with some bad white wine. When Louis returned, however, he felt very uncomfortable sitting at the superintendent's table.

"Well?"

"Désiré went to the Lion d'Or."

"Did he talk to old Cadaver?"

"To who?"

"Never mind. It's a nickname we gave him. Did Désiré talk to him?"

"It didn't happen like that. The man you call Cadav . . . It sounds really odd to me . . ."

"His name is Justin Cavre . . ."

"Monsieur Cavre, according to Liboureau, spent a good part of the evening watching the card players and saying nothing. Désiré was drinking in his usual corner. He left at about ten o'clock and a few minutes later Liboureau noticed that the Parisian had disappeared too. But he doesn't know if he left the inn or just went upstairs . . ."

"He left."

"What are you going to do?"

He was so proud to be working with the superintendent that he could not wait to get started.

"Who was it that reported seeing a considerable sum of money in Madame Retailleau's house?"

"The postman . . . Josaphat . . . Another drunkard . . . He's called Josaphat because when his wife died he had more to drink than usual and kept on saying through his tears: 'Goodbye, Céline . . . We'll meet again in the valley of Josaphat . . . Count on me . . .'"

"What would you like for dessert?" asked the *patronne*, who obviously had one of her children in her arms all day and worked with her one free hand. "I've biscuits or apples."

"Have which ever you like," said Maigret.

And the youngster replied, blushing:

"I don't mind . . . Some biscuits, please . . . This is what happened . . . about ten or twelve days after Albert's funeral, the postman went to collect some money from Madame Retailleau . . . She was busy doing the housework . . . She looked in her purse but she needed fifty francs more . . . So she walked over to the dresser, where the soup tureen is . . . You must have noticed it . . . It's got blue flowers on it . . . She stood in front of it so that Josaphat couldn't see what she was doing, but that evening, he swore he had seen some 1,000-franc notes, at least ten, he said, maybe more . . . Now, everybody knows that Madame Retailleau has never had as much money as that at one time . . . Albert spent all he earned . . ."

"What on?"

"He was rather vain . . . There's nothing wrong with that . . . He liked to be well-dressed and he had his suits made in Niort . . . He would often pay for a round of drinks, too . . . He would tell his mother that as long as she had her pension . . ."

"They quarreled, then?"

"Sometimes . . . Albert was an independent chap, you see . . . His mother would have liked to treat him like a little boy. If he had listened to her he would not have gone out at night and he'd never have set foot in the café . . . My mother's just the opposite . . . She's only too anxious to get me out of the house . . ."

"Where can we find Josaphat?"

"He'll probably be at home now, or else about to finish his first round. In half an hour he'll be at the station to collect the sacks with the second post . . ."

"Will you bring us some liqueurs please, madame?"

Through the curtains, Maigret stared at the windows on the other side of the street, imagined old Cadaver eating his lunch just as he was, and watching him likewise. It was not long before he realized his mistake, for a car ground noisily to a halt opposite the Lion d'Or and Cavre got out, his briefcase under his arm. Maigret watched him lean over toward the driver to find out how much he owed.

"Whose car is that?"

"It belongs to the man who owns the garage. We went

past it a little while ago. He acts as a taxi driver every now and again, if someone's ill and needs to be taken to hospital, or if someone wants something urgently . . ."

The car made a half turn and judging by the noise did not go far.

"You see. He's gone back to his garage."

"Do you get on well with him?"

"He's a friend of my boss."

"Go and ask him where he took his client this morning."

Less than five minutes later, Louis came running back.

"He went to Fontenay-le-Comte. It's exactly twenty-two kilometers from here . . ."

"Didn't you ask him where they went in Fontenay?"

"He was told to stop at the Café du Commerce, in the Rue de la République. The Parisian went in, came out with another man and told the driver to wait . . ."

"You don't know who this man was?"

"The garage man didn't know him . . . They were gone about half an hour . . . Then the man you call Cavre was driven back. He only gave a five franc tip . . ."

Had not Etienne Naud also gone to Fontenay-le-Comte?

"Let's go and see Josaphat . . ."

He had already left his house. They met up with him at the station where he was waiting for the train. When he saw young Louis with Maigret from the other end of the platform, he looked annoyed and went hurriedly into the station master's office, as if he had some business to attend to.

But Louis and Maigret waited for him to come out.

"Josaphat!" called out Louis.

"What do you want? I'm in a hurry . . ."

"There's a gentleman here who'd like a word with you."

"Who? I'm on duty and when I'm on duty . . ."

Maigret had the utmost difficulty in steering him toward an empty spot between the lamp room and the urinals.

"I just want an answer to a simple question . . ."

The postman was on his guard, that was obvious. He pretended he heard the train and was ready to rush off to the carriage carrying the mailbags. At the same time, he could not help glowering briefly at Louis for putting him in this position.

Maigret already knew he would get nothing out of him, that his colleague Cavre had already questioned him.

"Hurry up, I can hear the train . . ."

"About ten days ago, you called at Madame Retailleau's house to collect some money."

"I'm not allowed to discuss my work . . ."

"But you discussed it that very evening . . ."

"In front of me!" interjected the youngster. "Avrard was there, and so was Lhériteau and little Croman . . ."

The postman stood on one leg and then the other, with a stupid, insolent look on his face.

"What right have you to interrogate me?"

"We can ask you a question, can't we? You're not the Pope, are you?"

"And what if I asked him to show me his papers? He's been snooping round the neighborhood all morning!"

Maigret had already begun to walk away, knowing that it was pointless trying to discuss the matter further. Louis, however, lost his temper in the face of such blatant hostility.

"Do you mean you've the nerve to say you didn't tell everyone about the thousand franc notes you saw in the soup tureen?"

"I can say what I like, can't I? Or are you going to try and stop me?"

"You told everyone what you saw. I'll get the others to back me up, I'll get them to repeat what you said. You even said the notes were held together by a pin . . ."

The postman shrugged his shoulders and walked away. This time the train really was coming into the station and he walked down the platform to where the mail coach usually came to a halt.

"The swine!" growled Louis under his breath. "You heard what he said, didn't you? But you can take my word for it. Why should I lie? I knew perfectly well this would happen . . ."

"Why?"

"Because it's always the same with them . . ."

"With who?"

"With the lot of them . . . I can't really explain . . . They stick together . . . They're rich . . . They're either related to or else friends of magistrates, *préfets* and generals . . . I don't know whether you understand what I'm trying to say . . . So the townspeople are afraid . . . They often gossip at night when they've had a bit too much to drink and then regret it the next day . . .

"What are you going to do now? You're not going back to Paris, are you?"

"Of course not, son. Why do you ask?"

"I don't know. The other man looks . . ."

The youngster stopped himself just in time. He was probably about to say something like:

"The other man looks so much stronger than you!"

And it was true. Through the mist that was beginning to come down, as if it were dusk, Maigret thought he saw Cavre's face, his thin lips spreading into a sardonic smile.

"Isn't your boss going to be cross if you don't get back to your work?"

"Oh! No . . . He's not one of them . . . If he could help us prove poor Albert was murdered, he would, I promise you . . ."

Maigret jumped when a voice behind him asked:

"Could you tell me the way to the Lion d'Or, please?"

The railwayman on duty near the small gate pointed to the street which opened up about a hundred yards away.

"Go straight on . . . It's on your left, you'll see . . ."

A small, plump little man, faultlessly dressed and carrying a suitcase almost as large as himself, looked around for a non-existent porter. The superintendent examined him from head to foot, but his efforts were in vain. He had absolutely no idea who the stranger was.

5

THREE WOMEN IN A
DRAWING ROOM

Louis dived into the fog with his head bowed and before it enveloped him completely, he said to Maigret:

"If you want to get hold of me, I'll be at the Trois Mules all evening."

It was five o'clock. A thick fog had descended over the town and darkness fell at the same time. Maigret had to walk the length of the main street in Saint-Aubin in order to reach the station, where he would take the road leading to Etienne Naud's house. Louis had offered to go with him, but there is a limit to everything and Maigret had had enough. He was beginning to get tired of being pulled along by this excited and restless youngster.

As they parted company, Louis had said with a note of reproach in his voice, almost sentimentally:

"They'll butter you up and you'll start believing everything they tell you." He was referring to the Nauds, of course.

With his hands in his pockets and the collar of his overcoat turned up, Maigret walked cautiously toward the light in the distance, for any lamp which shone through the fog was a kind of lighthouse. Because of the intense brightness of this halo which looked as if it was still a long way off, the superintendent felt he was walking towards an important goal. And then, all of a sudden, he almost bumped into the cold window of the Vendée Cooperative which he had walked past twenty times that day. The narrow shop had been painted green fairly recently and there were free offers of glassware and earthenware displayed in the window.

Further on, in total darkness, he came up against something hard and groped about in confusion for some time before he realized he had landed in the middle of the carts standing outside the wheelwright's house with their shafts in the air.

The bells loomed into view immediately above his head. He was walking past the church. The post office was on the right, with its doll-size counter; opposite, on the other side of the road, stood the doctor's house.

The Lion d'Or was on one side of the street, the Trois Mules on the other. It was extraordinary to think that inside each lighted house people were living in a tiny circle of warmth, like incrustations in the icy infinity of the universe.

Saint-Aubin was not a large town. The lights in the dairy made one think of a brightly-lit factory at night. A railway engine in the station was sending out sparks.

Albert Retailleau had grown up in this microcosm of a world. His mother had spent all her life in Saint-Aubin.

Apart from holidays in Sables d'Olonne, someone like Geneviève Naud would to all intents and purposes never leave the town.

As the train slowed down a little before arriving at Niort station, Maigret had noticed empty streets in the rain, rows of gaslights and shuttered houses. He had thought to himself: "There are people who spend their whole lives in that street."

Testing the ground with his feet, he made his way along the canal towards another lighthouse which was in fact the lantern outside Naud's house. On various train journeys, whether on cold nights or in slashing rain, Maigret had seen many such isolated houses, a rectangle of yellow light being the only sign of their existence. The imagination then sets to work and pictures all manner of things.

And so it was that Maigret came into the orbit of one of these welcoming lights. He walked up the stone steps, looked for the bell and then saw that the door was ajar. He went into the hall, deliberately shuffling his feet to make his presence known, but this did not deter whoever was in the drawing room from continuing to hold forth in monotonous tones. Maigret took off his wet overcoat, his hat, wiped his feet on the straw mat and knocked on the door.

"Come in . . . Geneviève, open the door . . ."

He had already opened it; only one of the lamps in the drawing room was lit. Madame Naud was sewing by the hearth and a very old woman was sitting opposite her. A young girl walked over to the door as Maigret came into the room.

"I'm sorry to disturb you . . ."

The girl looked at him anxiously, unable to decide whether or not he would betray her. Maigret merely bowed.

"This is my daughter Geneviève, superintendent . . . She so wanted to meet you. She is quite recovered now . . . Allow me to introduce you to my mother . . ."

So this was Clémentine Bréjon, a La Noue before she married and commonly known as Tine. This small, sprightly old lady with a wry expression on her face reminiscent of that on the busts of Voltaire, rose to her feet and asked in a curious falsetto voice:

"Well, superintendent, do you feel you have caused enough havoc in our poor Saint-Aubin? Upon my word, I've seen you go up and down ten times or more this morning, and this afternoon I have it on good authority that you found yourself a young recruit . . . Do you know, Louise, who acted as elephant driver to the superintendent?"

Had she deliberately chosen the words "elephant driver" to emphasize the difference in size between the lanky youth and the elephantine Maigret?

Louise Naud, who was far from having her mother's vivacity and whose face was much longer and paler, did not look up from her work but just nodded her head and smiled faintly to show she was listening.

"Fillou's son . . . It was bound to happen . . . The boy must have lain in wait for him . . . No doubt he has regaled you with some fine stories, superintendent?"

"He has done nothing of the kind, madame . . . He merely directed me to the various people I wanted to see. I'd have found it difficult to find their houses on my own as the locals aren't exactly talkative on the whole . . ."

Geneviève had sat down and was staring at Maigret as if she was hypnotized by him. Madame Naud looked up occasionally from her work and glanced furtively at her daughter.

The drawing room looked exactly as it had done the previous evening for everything was in its usual place. An oppressive stillness hung over the room and it was really only the grandmother who conveyed any sense of normality.

"I am an old woman, superintendent. Let me tell you that, some time ago, something much more serious happened which nearly destroyed Saint-Aubin. There used to be a clog factory which employed fifty people, men and women. It was at a time when there were endless strikes in France and workers walked out at the slightest provocation."

Madame Naud had looked up from her work to listen and Maigret saw that she found it difficult to conceal her anxiety. Her thin face bore a striking resemblance to that of Bréjon the magistrate.

"One of the workmen in the clog factory was called Fillou. He wasn't a bad sort, but he was inclined to drink too much and when he was tipsy he thought he was a real orator. What happened exactly? One day, he went into the manager's office to lodge a complaint of some sort. Shortly afterwards the door opened. Fillou catapulted out, staggering backwards for several yards, and then fell into the canal."

"And he was the father of my young companion with the pock-marked face?" inquired Maigret.

"His father, yes. He is dead, now. At the time, the town was divided into two factions. One side thought that the drunken Fillou had behaved abominably and that the manager had been forced to take violent action to get rid of him. The other side felt that the manager was completely in the wrong and that he had provoked Fillou, taunting him when referring to the large families of his employees with remarks like:

"'I can't help it if they breed on Saturday nights when they're pissed . . .'"

"Fillou is dead, you said?"

"He died two years ago of cancer of the stomach."

"Did many people support him at the time of the incident?"

"The majority of people did not support him, but those who did were really committed to their cause.

Every morning various people used to find threats written in chalk on their doors."

"Are you implying, madame, that the case is similar to the one we are dealing with now?"

"I am not implying anything, superintendent. Old people love rambling on, you know. There is always some scandal or other to discuss in small towns. Life would be very dull, otherwise. And there will always be a few people willing to fan the flames . . ."

"What was the end of the Fillou affair?"

"Silence, of course . . ."

"Yes, silence just about sums it up," thought Maigret to himself. For despite the efforts of a few fanatics to stir things up, silence is always the most effective form of action. And he had been confronted with silence all day long.

Moreover, ever since he had come into the drawing room, a strange feeling had taken hold of him, a feeling which made him somewhat uneasy. He had trailed through the streets from morning till night, sullenly and obstinately following Louis, who had passed on to him something of his own eagerness.

"She's one of them . . ." Louis would say.

And "them" in Louis's mind meant a number of people who had conspired not to talk, and who did not want any trouble, people who wanted to let sleeping dogs lie.

In one sense, one could say that Maigret had sided with the small group of rebels. He had had a drink with

them at the Trois Mules. He had disowned the Nauds
when he declared he was not working for them and
whenever Louis doubted his word, he was sorely tempted
to give him proof of his loyalty.

And yet Louis had been right to look at the superintendent suspiciously when he left him, for he had an
inkling what would happen when his companion became the enemy's guest once again. That was why he
had tried his best to escort Maigret all the way to the
Nauds' front door, to bolster him up and caution him not
to give in.

"I'll be at the Trois Mules all evening, if you need
me . . ."

He would wait in vain. Now that he was back in
this cozy, bourgeois drawing-room, Maigret felt almost
ashamed of himself for having wandered through the
streets with a youngster and for having been snubbed
by everyone he had persisted in questioning.

There was a portrait on the wall which Maigret had
not noticed the night before, a portrait of Bréjon the examining magistrate, who seemed to be staring down at
the superintendent as if to say: "Don't forget the purpose of your visit."

He looked at Louise Naud's fingers as she sewed and
was hypnotized by their nervousness. Her face remained
almost serene, but her fingers revealed a fear which bor-
dered on panic.

"What do you think of our doctor?" asked the talkative old lady. "He's a real character, isn't he? You

Parisians are wrong in thinking no one of interest lives in the country. If you were to stay here for two months, no more . . . Louise, isn't your husband coming back?"

"He telephoned a short while ago to say he will be late. He's been called to La Roche-sur-Yon. He asked me to apologize on his behalf, superintendent . . ."

"I owe you an apology, too, for not having come back for lunch."

"Geneviève! Would you give the superintendent an apéritif . . ."

"Well, children, I must be going."

"Stay to dinner, *maman*. Etienne will take you home in the car when he gets back."

"I won't hear of it, my child. I don't need anyone to drive me home."

Her daughter helped her tie the ribbons of a small black bonnet which sat jauntily on her head and gave her galoshes to wear over her shoes.

"Would you like me to have the horse harnessed for you?"

"Time enough for that the day of my funeral. Goodbye, superintendent. If you're passing my house again, come in and see me. Goodnight, Louise. Goodnight, Vièvre . . ."

And suddenly the door was closed once more and a great feeling of emptiness prevailed. Maigret now understood why they tried to make old Tine stay. Now that she had gone, an oppressive, uneasy silence fell over the room and one sensed an aura of fear. Louise Naud's fingers ran increasingly rapidly over her work, while the young girl desperately tried to find an excuse to leave the room but did not dare.

Was it not an incredible thought that although Albert Retailleau was dead, although he had been discovered one morning, cut to pieces on the railway line, his son was living in this room at this very moment, in the form of a creature that would come into the world in a few months' time?

When Maigret turned towards the young girl, she did not look away. On the contrary, she stood up straight and looked Maigret squarely in the eye, as if to say:

"No, you did not dream it. I came into your bedroom last night and I wasn't sleepwalking. What I told you then is the truth. You see I am not ashamed of it. I am not mad. Albert was my lover and I am expecting his child . . ."

Albert, the son of Madame Retailleau, a woman who had stood up for her rights so bravely after her husband's death, Albert, Louis's young and faithful friend, used to creep into this house at night without anyone knowing. And Geneviève would take him into her room, the one at the end of the right wing of the house.

"Will you excuse me, ladies. I should like to go for a short walk round the stableyards, if you have no objection, that is . . ."

"May I come with you?"

"You'll catch cold, Geneviève."

"No, I won't, *maman*. I'll wrap up warmly."

She went into the kitchen to fetch a hurricane lamp which she brought back lit. In the hall, Maigret helped her on with her cape.

"What would you like to see?" she asked in a low voice.

"Let's go into the yard."

"We can go out this way. There's no point in going right around the house . . . Mind the steps . . ."

Lights were on in the stables whose doors were open, but the fog was so thick that one could not see anything.

"Your room is the one directly above us, isn't it?"

"Yes . . . I know what you are getting at . . . He didn't come in through the door, naturally . . . Come with me . . . You see this ladder . . . It's always left here . . . He just had to push it a few yards . . ."

"Which is your parents' room?"

"Three windows along."

"And the other two windows?"

"One is the spare bedroom, where Alban slept last night. The other is a room which hasn't been used since my little sister died, and *maman* has the key."

She was cold; she tried not to show it in order not to look as if she wanted to end the conversation.

"Your mother and father never suspected anything?"

"No."

"Had this affair been going on for some time?"

She answered at once.

"Three and a half months."

"Was Retailleau aware of the consequences of these meetings?"

"Yes."

"What did he intend to do?"

"He was going to tell my parents everything and marry me."

"Why was he angry, that last evening?"

Maigret looked at her closely, trying his best to glimpse the expression on her face through the fog. The ensuing silence betrayed the young girl's amazement.

"I asked you . . ."

"I heard what you said."

"Well!"

"I don't understand. Why do you say he was angry . . ."

And her hands trembled like her mother's, thereby causing the lantern to shake.

"Nothing out of the ordinary happened between you that night?"

"No, nothing."

"Did Albert leave by the window as usual?"

"Yes . . . There was a moon . . . I saw him go over to the back of the yard where he could jump over the little wall on to the road."

"What time was it?"

"About half past twelve."

"Did he usually stay for such a short time?"

"What do you mean?"

She was playing for time. Behind a window, not far from where they were standing, they could see the old cook moving about.

"He arrived at about midnight. I imagine he usually stayed longer . . . You didn't have a fight?"

"Why should we have had a fight?"

"I don't know . . . I'm just asking . . ."

"No . . ."

"When was he to speak to your parents?"

"Soon . . . We were waiting for a suitable moment . . ."

"Try to remember accurately . . . Are you sure there were no lights on in the house that night? You heard no noise? There was no one skulking in the yard?"

"I didn't see anything . . . I swear to you, superintendent, I know nothing . . . Maybe you don't believe me, but it's the truth . . . I'll never, do you hear, never tell my father what I told you last night . . . I shall leave. I don't yet know what I'll do . . ."

"Why did you tell me?"

"I don't know . . . I was frightened . . . I thought you would find out everything and tell my parents . . ."

"Shall we go back? You're shivering."

"You won't say anything?"

He did not know what to say. He did not want to be bound by a promise. He muttered:

"Trust me."

Was he, too, "one of them," to use Louis's phrase? Oh! Now he understood perfectly what the youngster meant. Albert Retailleau was dead and buried. A certain number of people in Saint-Aubin, the majority in fact, thought that since it was impossible to bring the young man back to life, the wisest course of action was to treat the subject as closed.

To be "one of them" was to belong to that tribe. Even Albert's mother was "one of them" since she had not appeared to understand why anyone should wish to investigate her son's death.

And those who had not subscribed to this view at the outset had been brought to heel one after the other. Désiré wished he had never found the cap. What cap? He now had money to drink his fill and could send a money order for five hundred francs to his good-for-nothing son.

Josaphat, the postman, could not remember having seen a wad of thousand franc notes in the soup tureen.

Etienne Naud was embarrassed that his brother-in-law should have thought of sending someone like Maigret, a man bent on discovering the truth.

But what was the truth? And who stood to gain by discovering the truth? What good would it do?

The small group of men in the Trois Mules, a carpenter, a plowman and a youngster called Louis Fillou whose father had already proved to be strong-willed, were the only ones to weave stories round the affair.

"Aren't you hungry, superintendent?" asked Madame Naud, as Maigret came into the drawing-room. "Where is my daughter?"

"She was in the hall just now. I expect she has gone up to her room for a minute."

The atmosphere for the next quarter of an hour was gloomy indeed. Maigret and Louise Naud were now alone in the old-fashioned, stuffy drawing room. From time to time a log toppled over and sent sparks flying into the grate. The single lamp with its pink shade shed a soft glow over the furniture. Familiar sounds coming from the kitchen occasionally broke the silence. They could hear the stove being filled with coal, a saucepan being moved, an earthenware plate being put on the table.

Maigret sensed that Louise Naud would have liked to talk. She was possessed by a demon who was pushing her to say . . . To say what? She was in considerable difficulty. Sometimes she would open her mouth, as if she had decided to speak, and Maigret would be afraid of what she was going to say.

She said nothing. Her chest tightened in a nervous spasm and her shoulders shook for a second. She went on with her embroidery, making tiny stitches, as if weighed down by this cloak of silence and stillness which formed such a barrier between them.

Did she know that Retailleau and her daughter . . .

"Do you mind if I smoke, madame?"

She gave a start. Perhaps she had been afraid he was going to say something else. She stammered:

"Please do . . . Make yourself at home . . ."

Then she sat up straight and listened for a sound.

"Oh, my goodness . . ."

Oh, my goodness what? She was merely waiting for her husband to return, waiting for someone to come and end the torment of this tête-à-tête.

And then Maigret began to feel sorry for her. What was to stop him getting up and saying:

"I think your brother made a mistake in asking me to come here. There is nothing I can do. This whole affair is none of my business and, if you don't mind, I'll take the next train back to Paris. I am most grateful to you for your hospitality."

He recalled Louis's pale face, his fiery eyes, the rueful smile on his lips. Above all, he pictured Cavre with his briefcase under his arm, Cavre who after all these years had suddenly been given the chance to get the better of his loathsome ex-boss. For Cavre hated him, there was no doubt about that. Admittedly, he hated everyone, but he hated Maigret in particular, for Maigret was his *alter ego*, a successful version of his own self.

Cavre had doubtless been up to all sorts of shady tricks ever since he got off the train the night before and was nearly mistaken by Naud for Maigret himself.

Where was the clock which was going tick-tock?

Maigret looked round for it. He felt really uncomfort-able and said to himself:

"Another five minutes and this poor woman's nerves will get the better of her . . . She'll make a clean breast of it . . . She can't stand it any longer . . . She's at the end of her tether . . ."

All he had to do was ask her one specific question. Hardly that! He would go up to her and look at her searchingly. Would she be able to restrain herself then?

But instead, he remained silent and even timidly picked up a magazine which was lying on a small round table to put her at her ease. It was a women's magazine full of embroidery patterns.

Just as in a dentist's waiting-room one reads things one would never read anywhere else, Maigret turned the pages and looked carefully at the pink and blue pic-tures, but the invisible chain which bound him to his hostess remained as tight as ever.

They were saved by the entry of the maid. She was rather a rough-looking country girl whose black dress and white apron merely accentuated her rugged, irreg-ular features.

"Oh! *Pardon* . . . I didn't know there was someone . . ."

"What is it, Marthe?"

"I wanted to know if I should lay the table or wait for monsieur . . ."

"Lay the table!"

"Will Monsieur Alban be here for dinner?"

"I don't know. But lay his place as usual . . ."

What a relief to talk of everyday things, they were so simple and reassuring! She latched on to Alban as a topic of conversation.

"He came to lunch here today. It was he who answered the telephone when you rang . . . He leads such a lonely life! We consider him one of the family now . . ."

The maid's appearance had given her a golden opportunity to escape and she made the most of it.

"Will you excuse me for a moment? You know what it's like to be mistress of the house. There is always something to see to in the kitchen . . . I'll ask the maid to tell my daughter to come down and keep you company . . ."

"Please don't bother . . ."

"Besides . . ." She listened carefully to see if she could hear anything. "Yes . . . That must be my husband . . ."

A car drew up in front of the steps, but the engine went on running. They heard voices and Maigret wondered whether his host had brought someone back with him, but he was only giving instructions to a servant who had rushed outside on hearing the car.

Naud came into the drawing-room still wearing his suede coat. There was an anxious look in his eyes as he surveyed Maigret and his wife, astonished to find them alone together.

"Ah! You're . . ."

"I was just saying to the superintendent, Etienne, that I would have to leave him for a minute and see to things in the kitchen . . ."

"Forgive me, superintendent . . . I am on the board of the regional agricultural authority and I had forgotten we had an important meeting today."

He sneezed and poured himself a glass of *porto,* trying all the while to gauge what could have happened in his absence.

"Well, have you had a good day? I was told on the telephone you were too busy to come back for lunch . . ."

He, too, was afraid of being alone with the superintendent. He looked round at the armchairs in the drawing-room, as if to reproach them for being empty.

"Alban's not here yet?" he said with a forced smile, turning towards the dining-room door which was still open.

And his wife answered from the kitchen:

"He came to lunch. He didn't say whether he'd be here for dinner . . ."

"Where's Geneviève?"

"She went up to her room."

He did not dare sit down and settle himself in a chair. Maigret understood how he felt and almost came to share his anxiety. In order to feel strong, or in order not to tremble visibly, the three of them needed to be together, side by side, in an unbroken family circle.

Only then would the superintendent be able to sense the spirit of the house in normal times. The two men helped each other, for they talked of seemingly trivial things and the sound of their chatter reassured them both.

"Will you have a glass of *porto?*"

"I have just had one."

"Well, have another . . . Now . . . Tell me what you've been doing . . . Or rather . . . For perhaps I am being indiscreet . . ."

"The cap has disappeared," declared Maigret, his eyes on the carpet.

"Has it really? This famous cap was to be proof . . . And where was it . . . Mind you, I have always had my doubts as to whether it really existed . . ."

"A young lad called Louis Fillou claims it was in one of the drawers in his bedroom . . ."

"In Louis's house? And you mean it was stolen this morning? Don't you think that is rather odd?"

He stood there laughing, a tall, strong, sturdy figure of a man with a ruddy complexion. He was the owner of this house, the head of the family, and he had just taken part in administrative debates in La Roche-sur-Yon. He was Etienne Naud, Squire Naud as the locals would have said, the son of Sébastien Naud who was known and respected by everyone in the *département*.

But his laughter sounded shaky as he took a glass of port and looked round in vain for a member of his family to appear. At a time like this, he needed the support they always gave him. He would have liked them to be present, his wife, his daughter and even Alban, who had decided to stay away today of all days.

"Will you have a cigar? . . . No, are you sure?"

He walked around and around the room, as though to sit down would have been to fall into a trap, to play right into the hands of the formidable superintendent whom that idiotic brother-in-law of his had foisted on him. Etienne Naud felt doomed.

6

ALBAN GROULT-COTELLE'S ALIBI

Before dinner that evening, an incident occurred which, though insignificant in itself, nonetheless gave Maigret food for thought. Etienne Naud had still not sat down, as though afraid of being even more at the mercy of the superintendent if he were once to remain still. They could hear voices in the dining room. Madame Naud was reprimanding the maid for not cleaning the silver properly. Geneviève had just come downstairs.

Maigret saw the look her father gave her as she came into the drawing room. There was a trace of anxiety in his expression. Naud had not seen his daughter since she had retired to her room the day before, saying she did not feel well. It was perfectly natural, too, that Geneviève should reassure him with a smile.

Just at that moment the telephone rang and Naud went into the hall to answer it. He left the drawing room door open.

"What?" he said, in an astonished tone of voice. "Of course he's here, damn it. What did you say? . . . Yes, hurry up, we're expecting you . . ."

When he came back into the drawing room he shrugged his shoulders once again.

"I wonder what has got into our friend Alban. There's been a place for him at our table for years. Then he rings up this evening to find out if you're here and when I say you are he asks if he can come to dinner and says he must talk to you . . ."

By chance, Maigret happened to be looking, not at Naud but at his daughter, and he was surprised to see such a fierce expression on her face.

"He did more or less the same thing earlier on," she said crossly. "He came here to lunch and looked very peeved when he realized the superintendent hadn't come back. I thought he was going to leave. He muttered: 'What a pity. I had something to show him.'

"He took his leave as soon as he had gulped down his dessert. You must have met him in the town, then, superintendent?"

Whatever it was was so subtle that Maigret could not pinpoint it. A hint of something in the young girl's voice. And yet it was not really the voice. What is it, for example, that makes an experienced man suddenly realize that a young girl has become a woman?

Maigret noticed something of this sort. It seemed to him that Geneviève's peevish words displayed something more than plain ill temper, and he decided to watch young Mademoiselle Naud more closely.

Madame Naud came in, apologizing for her absence. Her daughter availed herself of the opportunity to repeat:

"Alban has just rung to say he's coming to dinner. But first of all he asked whether the superintendent was here. He's not coming to see *us* . . ."

"He'll be here in a minute," said her father who had finally sat down, now that his family was round him. "It will take him three minutes by bicycle."

Maigret dutifully remained seated, looking rather dejected. His large eyes were expressionless as they always were whenever he found himself in an awkward situation. He watched them in turn, smiling slightly when spoken to, and all the while thinking to himself:

"They must be cursing their idiot of a brother-in-law and me, too. They all know what happened, including their friend Alban. That's why they are jittery the minute they are on their own. They feel reassured when they are together and gang up . . ."

What had happened, in fact? Had Etienne Naud discovered the young Retailleau in his daughter's bedroom? Had they quarreled? Had they had a fight? Or had Naud quite simply shot him down like he would a rabbit?

What a night to have lived through! Geneviève's mother must have been in a terrible state and the servants who probably heard the noise must have been petrified.

Someone was scraping his feet at the front door. Geneviève made a move, as if to go and open the door, but then decided to remain seated and Naud himself, somewhat surprised, as if his daughter's behavior constituted a serious breach of habit, got up and went into the hall. Maigret heard him talking about the fog and then the two men came into the drawing room.

This was the first time, in fact, that Maigret had seen Geneviève and Alban together. She held out her hand rather stiffly. Alban bowed, kissed the back of her hand and then turned towards Maigret, obviously anxious to tell him or show him something.

"Would you believe, superintendent, that after you left this morning I came across this quite by chance . . ."

And he held out a small sheet of paper which had been attached to some others with a pin, for there were two tiny prick marks in it.

"What is it?" asked Naud quite naturally, while his daughter looked distrustfully at Alban.

"You have all made fun of my mania for hoarding the smallest scrap of paper. I could produce the tiniest laundry bill dated three or eight years back!"

The piece of paper that Maigret kept twirling between his fat fingers was a bill from the Hôtel de l'Europe in La Roche-sur-Yon. *Room: 30 francs. Breakfast: 6 francs. Service* . . . The date: *January 7*.

"Of course," said Alban, as though he were apologizing, "it's not important. However, I remembered the police like alibis. Look at the date. Quite by chance, I was in La Roche, do you see, on the night the person you know met his death . . ."

Naud and his wife reacted as well-bred people do when confronted with a breach of manners. Unable to believe her ears, Madame Naud looked first at Alban, as though she would not have expected such behavior from him, and then looked down with a sigh at the logs in the grate. Her husband frowned. He was slower on the uptake. Perhaps he was hunting for some deeper meaning to his friend's ploy?

As for Geneviève, she had turned pale with anger. She had obviously had a real shock, and the pupils of her eyes glistened. Maigret had been so intrigued by her behavior a few moments before that he tried not to look at anyone else.

Alban, with his thin, lanky physique and balding forehead, stood sheepishly in the middle of the drawing room.

"At any rate, you're making quite sure you are in the clear before you are accused," said Naud when he finally spoke, having had time to weigh his words.

"What do you mean by that, Etienne? I think you have all misinterpreted me. I came across this hotel bill quite by chance when I was sorting out some papers a short while ago. I was eager to show it to the superintendent as it was such a strange coincidence it had the same date on it as the day . . ."

Madame Naud even chipped in, something that rarely happened.

"So you've already said," she retorted. "I think dinner is ready now . . ."

The atmosphere was still strained. Although the meal was as elaborate and well-cooked as it had been

on the previous evening, their efforts to create a friendly
ambience or at any rate an outward show of relaxation
failed dismally. Geneviève was the most agitated. For a
long time afterwards Maigret could still picture her, her
chest heaving with emotion: a woman's anger but also a
mistress's rage, Maigret was sure. She pecked at her
food, disdainfully. Not once did she look at Alban who,
for his part, made sure he caught no one's eye.

Alban was just the sort of man to keep the smallest
scraps of paper and file them away, pinning them together
in bundles as if they were banknotes. It was also just like
him to get himself out of difficulty if he had the chance
and with a clear conscience leave his friends in hot water.

All this made itself felt. There was something scan-
dalous afoot. Madame Naud looked even more anxious.
Naud, on the other hand, endeavored to reassure his
family, although quite probably with another objective
in mind.

"By the way, I happened to meet the Director of
Prosecutions in Fontenay this morning. In fact, Alban,
he is almost a relative of yours through the female side,
as he married a Deharme, from Cholet."

"The Cholet Deharmes aren't related to the general's
family. They originally came from Nantes and their . . ."

Naud went on:

"He was most reassuring, you know, superintendent.
Admittedly, he has told my brother-in-law Bréjon that
there is bound to be an official inquiry, but it will just be

a formality, at any rate as far as we are concerned. I told him you were here . . ."

Well! He immediately regretted making this thought-less comment. He blushed slightly, and hurriedly put a large piece of lobster *à la crème* into his mouth.

"What did he have to say about that?"

"He admires you greatly and has followed most of your cases in the newspapers. It is precisely because he admires you . . ."

The poor man did not know how to extricate himself.

"He is amazed that my brother-in-law deemed it necessary to involve a man like you in such a trivial matter . . ."

"I understand . . ."

"You're not angry, I hope? He only said this because of his admiration for . . ."

"Are you sure he didn't also say that my appearance here may well make the case seem more important than it actually is?"

"How did you know? Have you seen him?"

Maigret smiled. What else could he do? For was he not a guest in their house? The Nauds had entertained him as well as they could. And again, that night, the dinner they served was a small but consummate example of traditional provincial cooking.

In a pleasant, very polite way, his hosts now began to make him feel that his presence in their midst was a threat, a potentially harmful factor.

There was silence, as there had been a short while before, after the Alban episode. It was Madame Naud who tried to put things right and she made a bigger blunder than her husband had done.

"At any rate, I hope you'll stay a few more days with us? I expect there will be a frost after the fog has gone and you will be able to go on some walks with my husband . . . Don't you think, Etienne?"

How relieved they all would have been if Maigret had replied as they assumed he would, in the manner of a well-bred man:

"I would gladly stay, and greatly appreciate your hospitality, but alas I must return to my duties in Paris. I may pass this way in the holidays . . . But I have enjoyed myself enormously . . ."

He said nothing of the kind. He went on eating and did not reply. Inwardly, he felt a brute. These people had behaved well towards him from the outset. Perhaps Albert Retailleau's death weighed heavily on their conscience? But had not the young man robbed their daughter of her honor, as the saying goes in their circles? And had Albert's mother, Madame Retailleau, made a fuss? Or had she been the first to realize that it was far better to let sleeping dogs lie?

Three or four people, perhaps more, were trying to keep their secret, desperately trying to prevent anyone from discovering the truth, and for someone like Madame Naud, Maigret's presence alone must have been an intolerable strain. Had she not been on the point of crying out in anguish a short while ago, at the end of quarter of an hour alone with the superintendent?

It was so simple! He would leave the following morning with the whole family's blessing and, back in Paris, Bréjon the examining magistrate would thank him with tears in his eyes!

And if Maigret did not take this course of action, was it his passion for justice alone which prompted him to do otherwise? He would not have dared look someone in the eye and say this was so. For there was Cavre. There were the successive rebuttals Cavre had inflicted on him ever since their arrival the night before, without so much as a glance in the direction of his former boss. He came and went as if Maigret did not exist, or as if he were a totally innocuous opponent.

Whenever Maigret passed by, as though by magic, evidence melted away, witnesses could remember nothing or refused to speak, and items of unmistakable proof, like the cap, vanished into thin air.

At last, after so many years, the wretched, unlucky, grudging Cavre had his moment of triumph!

"What are you thinking about, superintendent?"

He gave a start.

"Nothing . . . I'm so sorry. My mind wanders sometimes . . ."

He had helped himself to a huge plateful of food without realizing what he was doing and was now ashamed of himself. To put him at his ease, Madame Naud said quietly:

"Nothing gives more pleasure to the mistress of the house than to see her cooking appreciated. Alban eats like a wolf so it doesn't count, as he'd eat anything put in front of him. Everything tastes good to him. He's not a gourmet. He's a glutton."

She was joking, of course, but nonetheless there was a trace of spite in her voice and expression.

A few glasses of wine had made Etienne Naud's face even rosier. Playing with his knife, he ventured:

"So what do you make of it all, superintendent, now that you've seen something of the neighborhood and have asked a few questions?"

"He has met young Fillou . . ." his wife informed him, as though in warning.

And Maigret, whom each of them was watching like a hawk, said slowly and clearly:

"I think Albert Retailleau was very unlucky . . ."

The remark did not really imply anything and yet Geneviève grew pale, indeed seemed so taken aback by these few insignificant words that for a moment she looked as if she would get up and leave the room. Her father looked puzzled, unsure of what Maigret meant. Alban sneered:

"I reckon that's a statement worthy of the ancient oracles! I'd certainly be very uneasy if I hadn't miraculously found proof that I was sleeping peacefully in a room in the Hôtel de l'Europe eighty kilometers from here, on that very night . . ."

"Don't you know," retorted Maigret, "that there is a

saying in the police force that he who has the best alibi is all the more suspect?"

Alban was annoyed. Taking Maigret's little joke seriously, he answered:

"Then in that case, you will have to hold the *préfet*'s private secretary suspect too, as he spent the evening with me. He is a childhood friend of mine whom I see from time to time and whenever we spend an evening together we don't usually get to bed until two or three in the morning . . ."

What made Maigret decide to carry on the pretense to the end? Was it the blatant cowardice of this trumped-up aristocrat which spurred him to act thus? He took a large notebook with an elastic band round it out of his pocket and asked with all seriousness:

"What is his name?"

"Do you really want it? As you wish . . . Musellier . . . Pierre Musellier . . . He has remained a bachelor . . . He has a flat in the Place Napoléon, above the Murs garages . . . About fifty yards from the Hôtel de l'Europe . . ."

"Shall we have coffee in the drawing room?" suggested Madame Naud. "Will you serve the coffee, Geneviève? You're not too tired? You look pale to me. Do you think you had better go upstairs to bed?"

"No."

She was not tired. She was tense. It was as if she had various accounts to settle with Alban, for she did not take her eyes off him.

"Did you return to Saint-Aubin the following morning?" asked Maigret, with a pencil in his hand.

"The very next morning, yes. A friend gave me a lift in his car to Fontenay-le-Comte, where I had lunch with some other friends, and just as I was leaving I bumped into Etienne who brought me back."

"You go from friend to friend, in effect . . ."

He could not have made it clearer that he thought Alban was a sponger and it was true. Everyone understood perfectly the implications of Maigret's words. Geneviève blushed and looked away.

"Are you sure you won't change your mind and have one of my cigars, superintendent?"

"Would you be so kind as to tell me if you have finished questioning me? If you have, I would like to take my leave . . . I want to get home early tonight."

"That's absolutely fine. In fact, I'd like to walk as far as the town so if it's all right with you, we can go together . . ."

"I came by bicycle . . ."

"That doesn't matter . . . A bicycle can be pushed by hand, can't it? And anyway, you might bicycle into the canal in this fog . . ."

What *was* going on? For one thing, when Maigret had talked of leaving with Alban Groult-Cotelle, Etienne Naud had frowned and appeared to be on the point of accompanying them.

Did he fear that Alban, who was far too nervous that night, might be tempted to confess all? He had given him a long look, as if to say: "For heavens's sake, be careful! Look how het-up you are. He is tougher than you . . ."

Geneviève gave Alban an even sterner, more contemptuous look which said: "At least try and control yourself!"

Madame Naud did not look at anyone. She was weary. She no longer understood what was going on. It would not be long before she gave way under such nervous tension.

But the person who behaved most strangely of all was Alban himself. He would not make up his mind to go but walked around the drawing room, his intention in all probability being to have a private talk with Naud.

"Did you not want a word with me in your study about that insurance matter?"

"What insurance matter?" said Naud stupidly.

"Not to worry. We'll talk about it tomorrow."

What did he want to tell Naud that was so important?

"Are you coming, my dear fellow?" persisted the superintendent.

"Are you sure you don't want me to take you in the car? If you would like to have the car and drive yourself . . ."

"No thank you. We'll have a good chat as we walk . . ."

The fog swirled round them. Alban pushed his bicycle with one hand and walked quickly along, constantly having to stop because Maigret would not walk more briskly.

"They are such good sorts! Such a united family . . . But it must be rather a dull life for a young girl, mustn't it? Has she many friends?"

"I don't know of any in the neighborhood . . . Every now and then she goes off to spend a week or so with her cousins and they come down here in the summer, but apart from that . . ."

"I imagine she also goes and stays with the Bréjons in Paris?"

"Yes, indeed, she stayed with them this winter."

Maigret changed the subject, playing the innocent. The two men could scarcely see each other in the icy white mist that enveloped them. The electric light in the station acted as a lighthouse and, further on, two more lights which could have been boats out to sea, shone through the haze.

"So apart from staying in La Roche-sur-Yon from time to time, you hardly ever leave Saint-Aubin?"

"I sometimes go to Nantes as I have friends there, and also to Bordeaux where my cousin from Chièvre lives. Her husband is a shipowner."

"Do you ever go to Paris?"

"I was there a month ago."

"At the same time as Mademoiselle Naud?"

"Perhaps. I really don't know . . ."

They walked past the two inns opposite each other. Maigret stopped and suggested:

"What about having a drink in the Lion d'Or? It would be most interesting to see my old colleague

Cavre. I saw a young fellow at the station just now and I suspect he has been asked to come to the rescue."

"I'll take my leave, then . . ." said Alban quickly.

"No, no . . . If you don't want to stop, I'll keep you company on your way home. You can't object to that, now, can you?"

"I am in a hurry to get back and go to bed. I'll be quite open with you . . . I am prone to the most dreadful migraines and I am in the throes of one now."

"All the more reason to escort you home. Does your maid sleep in the house?"

"Of course."

"Some people don't like their servants to be under the same roof at night . . . Look! There's a light . . ."

"It's the maid . . ."

"Is she in the sitting room? Of course, the room is heated . . . Does she do odd sewing jobs for you when you are out?"

They stopped outside the front door and Alban, instead of knocking, hunted in his pocket for the key.

"See you tomorrow, superintendent! No doubt we will meet at my friends the Nauds . . ."

"Tell me . . ."

Alban took care not to open the door lest Maigret would think he was inviting him inside.

"It's stupid . . . Please forgive me . . . But I am afraid I've been taken short, and since we're here . . . We men can be honest with each other, can't we?"

"Come in . . . I'll show you the way . . ."

The light was not on in the corridor but the sitting-room door on the left was half-open and revealed a rectangle of light. Alban tried to lead Maigret down the corridor but the superintendent, in an almost instinctive gesture, pushed the door wide-open, whereupon he stopped in his tracks and cried out:

"Well I never! It's my old friend Cavre! What are you doing here, my dear chap?"

The ex-inspector had risen to his feet, looking as pale and sullen as ever. He glowered at Groult-Cotelle whom he deemed responsible for this disastrous meeting.

Alban was completely out of his depth. He tried hard to think of an explanation but, unable to do so, merely asked:

"Where is the maid?"

Old Cadaverous was the first to regain his composure and bowing, said:

"Monsieur Groult-Cotelle, I think?"

Alban was slow to understand the inspector's game.

"I am sorry to disturb you at such an hour, but I just wanted a few words with you. Since your maid told me you would not be back late . . ."

"All right!" growled Maigret.

"What?" said Alban with a start.

"I said: All right!"

"What do you mean?"

"I don't mean anything. Cavre, where is this maid who showed you in? There is no other light on in the house. In other words, she was in bed."

"She told me . . ."

"All right! I'll try once more, and this time I don't want any clap-trap. You can sit down, Cavre. Now! You made yourself comfortable. You took off your over-coat and left your hat on the coat stand. What were you in the middle of reading?"

Maigret's eyes opened wide when he inspected the book lying on the table near Cavre's chair.

"*Sexual Perversions!* Look at that, now! And you found this charming book in the library of our friend Groult-Cotelle . . . Tell me, gentlemen, why don't you sit down? Does my presence disturb you? Don't forget your migraine, Monsieur Groult-Cotelle . . . You should take an aspirin."

In spite of everything, Alban still had enough presence of mind to retort:

"I thought you needed to relieve yourself?"

"Well, I don't anymore . . . Now, my dear Cavre, what is this investigation of yours all about? You must have been really put out when you realized I was in-volved in this too, eh?"

"Ah! You're involved? How do you mean, in-volved?"

"So Groult-Cotelle availed himself of your expertise, did he? Far be it for me to underrate it, by the way . . ."

"I had never even heard of Monsieur Groult-Cotelle until this morning."

"It was Etienne Naud who told you about him when you met in Fontenay-le-Comte, wasn't it?"

"Superintendent, if you wish to submit me to a formal interrogation, I would like my lawyer to be present when I answer your questions."

"In the event of your being accused of stealing a cap, for instance?"

"In that event, yes."

The electric light bulb cast a gray light over the sitting room for apart from the fact it was of insufficient strength for the size of the room, it was also coated in dust.

"May I perhaps be permitted to offer you something to drink?"

"Why not?" answered Maigret. "Seeing as fate has brought us together . . . By the way, Cavre, was it one of your men I saw just now at the station?"

"He works for me, yes."

"Renfort?"

"As you wish."

"Did you have important matters to settle with Monsieur Groult-Cotelle tonight?"

"I wanted to ask him one or two questions."

"If you wanted to see him about his alibi, you can rest assured. He thought of everything. He even kept his bill from the Hôtel de l'Europe."

Cavre, however, kept his nerve. He had sat down in the chair he had occupied before and, with his legs crossed and his morocco-leather briefcase on his lap, seemed to be biding his time, determined, one might have said, to have the last word. Groult-Cotelle, who had filled three glasses with armagnac, offered him one which he refused.

"No, thank you. I only drink water."

He had been teased a great deal about this at the Police Headquarters, an unintentionally cruel thing to do, since Cavre was not teetotaler by choice but because he suffered from a severe disorder of the liver.

"And what about you, superintendent?"

"Gladly!"

They fell silent. All three men appeared to be playing a strange kind of game, such as trying to see who could remain silent the longest without giving way. Alban had emptied his glass in one go and had poured himself another. He remained standing and from time to time pushed one of the books in his library back into place if it was out of line.

"Are you aware, monsieur," Cavre said to him at last in a quiet voice, icy calm, "that you are in your own house?"

"What do you mean?"

"That as master of the house you are at liberty to entertain whomever you think fit. I should have liked to talk to you alone, not in front of the superintendent. If you prefer his company to mine, I will be glad to take my leave and arrange a meeting for some other time."

"In short, the inspector is politely asking you to show one of us to the door forthwith."

"Gentlemen, I don't understand what this discussion is all about. Indeed this whole affair has nothing to do with me. I was in La Roche, as you know, when the boy died. Granted, I am a friend of the Nauds. I have been to their house a great deal. In a small town like ours, one's choice of friends is limited."

"Remember Saint Peter!"

"What do you mean?"

"That if you go on like this, you will have thrice denied your friends the Nauds before sunrise, assuming, of course, the fog allows the sun to rise."

"It is all very well for you to joke. My position is a delicate one, all the same. The Nauds frequently invite me to their house. Etienne is my friend, I don't deny the fact. But if you ask me what happened at the Nauds' that night, I don't know and what is more, I don't want to know. So I am the wrong person to question, that's all."

"Perhaps Mademoiselle Naud would be the best person to question, then? Incidentally, I wonder if you were aware that she was looking at you far from lovingly this evening. I got the distinct impression that she had a bone to pick with you."

"With me?"

"Especially when you handed me your hotel bill and tried with such style to save your own skin. She didn't think that was very nice, not nice at all. I would be on your guard she doesn't get her own back, if I were you . . ."

Alban forced a laugh.

"You are joking. Geneviève is a charming child who . . ."

What made Maigret suddenly decide to play his last card?

". . . who is three months pregnant," he let drop, moving closer to Alban.

"What . . . What did you say?"

As for Cavre, he was stunned. For the first time that day he no longer looked his confident self and stared at his former boss in spontaneous admiration.

"Were you unaware of the fact, Monsieur Groult-Cotelle?"

"Just what are you getting at?"

"Nothing . . . I am looking for . . . You want to know the truth, too, don't you? . . . Then we will try and find it together . . . Cavre has already laid his hands on the blood-stained cap which is proof enough of the crime . . . Where is that cap, Cavre?"

The inspector sunk deeper into his armchair and did not reply.

"I had better warn you that you will pay dearly for it if you've destroyed it . . . And now, I have the feeling that my presence is disturbing you . . . I will therefore take leave of you both . . . I presume I will see you for lunch tomorrow at your friends the Nauds, Monsieur Groult-Cotelle?"

He went out of the room. As soon as he had banged the front door shut he saw a thin figure standing close by.

"Is that you, superintendent?"

It was young Louis. Lying in wait behind the windows of the Trois Mules, he had doubtless seen the shadowy figures of Maigret and Alban as they went past. He had followed them.

"Do you know what they are saying, what everyone is saying in the town?"

His voice was trembling with anxiety and indignation.

"People are saying that *they* have got the better of you and that you are leaving on the three o'clock train tomorrow . . ."

And this had very nearly been the truth.

7

THE OLD POSTMISTRESS

An important contributing factor must have made Maigret more sensitive than usual at that particular moment. Scarcely had he walked out of Groult-Cotelle's front door and taken a few steps in the darkness, the fog clinging to his skin like a cold compress, when he suddenly stopped. Young Louis, who was walking beside him, asked:

"What's the matter, superintendent?"

Something had just occurred to Maigret and he was trying to follow the thought through. He was still mindful of the sound of voices, blurred but noisy, coming to him from behind the shutters of the house. At the same time, he understood why the youngster was alarmed: Maigret had stopped dead for no apparent reason in the middle of the pavement, like a heart patient who is immobilized by a sudden attack wherever he happens to be.

But this had nothing to do with Maigret's current preoccupations. He did, however, make a mental note:

"Ah! So there's a heart patient in Saint-Aubin . . ."

He was later to learn, in fact, that the old doctor had died of angina pectoris. For years people had become accustomed to seeing him suddenly stop thus in the middle of the street, rooted to the spot with his hand on his heart.

There was a violent argument going on inside the house, or at least the sound of angry voices gave this impression, but Maigret paid no attention. The pock-marked Louis, who thought he had discovered the cause of the superintendent's sudden halt, listened conscientiously. The louder the voices, the harder it was to make out the words. The noise sounded exactly like a record whirling round off-center, due to a second hole having been bored, and blaring out unintelligible sounds.

It was not because of this fight between Inspector Cavre and Alban Groult-Cotelle that Maigret stopped like this and looked round rather uncertainly, staring at nothing in particular.

The minute he left the house, an idea had occurred to him. It was not even an idea, but something vaguer, so vague that he was now striving to recapture the memory of it. Every now and then, an insignificant occurrence, usually a whiff of something barely caught, reminds us in the space of a second of a particular moment in our life. It is such a vivid sensation that we are gripped by it and want to cling to this living reminder of that moment. It disappears almost at once and with it all recollection of the experience. Try as we might, we end up wondering, for want of an answer to our questions, if it was not an unconscious evocation of a dream, or, who knows, of some pre-existent world?

Something struck Maigret the moment he banged the front door shut. He knew he was leaving behind two embarrassed and angry men. Brought together by fate that night, the two of them had one thing in common, although there was no rational explanation for this. Cavre made one think not of a bachelor, but of a husband who has been subjected to ridicule and looks woeful and abashed. Envy oozed out of every pore and envy can make one behave just as equivocally as certain hidden vices.

Deep down, Maigret did not bear him a grudge. He felt sorry for him. While relentlessly pursuing him, determined to get the better of his rival, Maigret nonetheless felt a kind of pity for this man who, after all, was nothing but a failure.

What was the connection between Cavre and Alban? The connection which exists between two completely different but equally sordid things. It was almost a question of color. Both men had something of the gray, greenish quality of moral and material dust.

Cavre exuded hatred. Alban Groult-Cotelle exuded panic and cowardice. His whole life had been run on the principle of cowardice. His wife had left him and taken the children with her. He had made no effort either to join them or bring them back. He probably had not suffered. He had selfishly reorganized his existence. A man of humble means, he lived in other people's homes, like the cuckoo. And if some misfortune befell his friends, he was the first to let them down.

And now Maigret suddenly recalled the trifling matter that had triggered off this train of thought: it was the book he had caught Cavre holding when they came into the room, one of those disgusting, erotic books that are sold under the counter in certain backrooms in the Faubourg Saint-Martin.

Groult-Cotelle kept books like this in his country library; Cavre came upon one of them seemingly quite by chance!

But there had been something else, and it was this something else that the superintendent was struggling to put his finger on. For a tenth of a second, perhaps, his mind had been lit up, as it were, by a glaring truth, but no sooner had he realized this than the thought vanished and all that remained was a vague impression. In reality, this was why he stood motionless like a heart patient trying to outwit his heart.

Maigret was trying to outwit his memory. He was hoping . . .

"What is that light?" he asked, however.

They were both standing still in the fog. A little way off, Maigret could see a large halo of white, diffuse light. He concentrated his thoughts on this material thing in order to give his intuition time to revive. He now knew the town. So where, then, was this light almost opposite Groult-Cotelle's house coming from?

"It isn't the post office, is it?"

"It's the window next door," replied Louis. "The postmistress's window. She sleeps badly and reads novels well into the night. Hers is always the last light to be switched off in Saint-Aubin . . ."

Now, he was still aware of the sound of angry voices. Groult-Cotelle was shouting the loudest, as if he point-blank refused to listen to reason. Cavre's voice was more ponderous, more imperious.

Why was Maigret strongly tempted to cross the street and press his face against the postmistress's window? She was doubtless sitting reading in her kitchen. Was it intuition? A moment afterwards, the thought had gone from his mind. He knew that Louis was looking at him anxiously and impatiently as he wondered what on earth was going on in his hero's head.

What was it he had sensed as he went out of the front door? . . . Well . . . First of all, Paris had come to mind . . . The books, the shops in the Faubourg Saint-Martin which sell those kind of books had made him think of Paris . . . Groult-Cotelle had gone to Paris . . . and Geneviève Naud must have been there at the same time . . .

Maigret could remember the look on Geneviève's face when Alban had produced his alibi in so unpleasant a manner. It had contained more than mere scorn. This time, a naked woman, not a young girl, stood before Alban . . . A mistress, suddenly aware of the baseness of . . .

He had just got to this point in his thoughts when an inkling of something else had flashed through his mind only to vanish again, leaving a vague memory of something rather nasty.

Yes, the whole affair was very different from what Maigret had initially envisaged. Up until now, he had only seen the bourgeois view of things, had witnessed a thoroughly bourgeois family's indignation upon discovering that a penniless youth with no prospects was making love to their daughter.

Had Naud shot him in a fit of anger? It was possible. Maigret almost pitied Naud, and especially his wife, who knew what had happened. She was desperately trying to control herself and overcome her terror. For her, every minute spent alone with the superintendent was a terrible ordeal.

But now, Etienne Naud and his wife ceased to be foremost in his mind.

What was the missing link between these thoughts? The dull, balding Alban had an alibi. Was this really just a fluke? Was it also just a fluke that he had suddenly come across that bill from the Hôtel de l'Europe?

No doubt he really had spent the night there. The superintendent was convinced of this, although he decided to check the fact all the same.

But why had he gone to La Roche-sur-Yon on that particular night? Had the *préfet*'s private secretary been expecting him?

"I must find out!" grumbled Maigret to himself.

He went on looking at the dim light in the house next door to the post office; he still had his tobacco pouch in one hand and his pipe, which he was too preoccupied to fill, in the other.

Albert Retailleau was angry . . .

Who had said that? None other but his young companion Louis, Albert's friend.

"Was he really angry?" the superintendent suddenly asked.

"Who?"

"Your friend Albert . . . You said that when he left you that last evening . . ."

"He was very het-up. He drank several brandies before going off to meet Geneviève . . ."

"He didn't tell you anything?"

"Wait . . . He said he probably wouldn't stay very long in this godforsaken neighborhood . . ."

"How long had he been Mademoiselle Naud's lover?"

"I don't know . . . Wait though . . . They weren't lovers in midsummer. They must have started sleeping together about the month of October . . ."

"He wasn't in love with her before that?"

"Well, if he was, he didn't talk to her . . ."

"Ssh . . ."

Maigret stood quite still and listened carefully. The sound of voices had died away and now, to his astonishment, the superintendent heard a different sound.

"It's the telephone!" he exclaimed.

He had recognized the familiar sound of country telephones. Someone was turning a handle to call the woman in the post office.

"Run and have a look through the postmistress's window . . . You'll get there quicker than I will . . ."

He was right. A second light went on, in the window next to the first. The postmistress had gone through a door which was slightly ajar into the post office.

Maigret took his time. He loathed running anywhere. Strangely enough, it was young Louis's presence that bothered him. He wanted to maintain a certain dignity in front of the youngster. He at last filled his pipe, lit it and walked slowly across the street.

"Well?"

"I knew she would listen in to the call," whispered Louis. "The old shrew always listens. The doctor even complained to La Roche about it once, but she still goes on doing it . . ."

They could see her through the window, a small woman dressed in black with dark hair and an ageless face. She had one hand on an earphone and held a plug in the other. The call must have come to an end at that very moment, for she moved the plugs into different holes and walked across the room to switch off the light.

"Do you think she would let us in?"

"If you knock on the little door at the back . . . This way . . . We'll go through the yard . . ."

They groped about in pitch darkness for a moment, edging their way past various tubs filled with washing. A cat jumped out of a dustbin.

"Mademoiselle Rinquet!" the youngster called out. "Will you open up for a minute . . ."

"What is it?"

"It's me, Louis . . . Will you open up for a minute, please . . ."

As soon as she had unbolted the door, Maigret stepped hurriedly inside for fear she might shut it again.

"There is nothing to be afraid of, mademoiselle . . ."

He was too tall and too bulky for the tiny post-mistress's tiny kitchen which was littered with embroidered tray cloths and knick-knacks made of cheap china or spun glass she had bought at various fairs.

"Groult-Cotelle has just made a call."

"How do you know?"

"He rang up his friend Naud . . . You listened in to their conversation."

Caught at fault, she defended herself awkwardly.

"But the post office is shut, monsieur. I'm not supposed to give anyone a line after nine o'clock. I sometimes do, though, as I'm here and like to be helpful . . ."

"What did he say?"

"Who?"

"Look, if you're not going to answer my questions with a good grace, I will have to come back tomorrow, officially this time, and draw up a written report which will go through the proper channels. Now, what did he say?"

"There were two of them on the line."

"At the same time?"

"Pretty much. They spoke together sometimes. It turned into a shouting match between the two of them and in the end I couldn't catch what they were saying . . . They must both have had an earpiece and were obviously pushing each other out of the way in front of the telephone."

"What did they say?"

"Monsieur Groult said first of all:

"'Listen, Etienne, this can't go on. The superintendent has just left. He came face to face with your man. I'm sure he knows everything and if you go on . . .'"

"Well?" said Maigret.

"Wait . . . The other man butted in.

"'Hello . . . Monsieur Naud? . . . Cavre speaking . . . Of course it's a great pity you didn't manage to detain him and prevent him from finding me here, but . . .'"

"'But I'm the one who is compromised,' yelled Monsieur Groult. 'I've had enough, do you hear, Etienne? Put an end to all this! Telephone your idiotic brother-in-law and tell him never to meddle in our affairs again. He's this wretched superintendent's superior in some respects and since he's the one who sent him down here, he must set about calling him back to Paris . . . So I'm warning you . . . if he is at your house the next time I come around, I'll . . .'

"'Hello! Hello!' shouted Monsieur Etienne, in a real state at the other end of the line. 'Are you still there, Monsieur Cavre? . . . Alban's got me all worried . . . Are you sure . . .'

"'Hello! . . . Cavre here . . . Will you be quiet, Monsieur Groult . . . Let me get a word in . . . Stop pushing me . . . Is that you, Monsieur Naud? . . . Yes . . . Well! There is nothing to worry about provided your friend Groult-Cotelle doesn't panic and . . . What? . . . Should you call your brother-in-law? . . . I'd have advised you not to a moment ago . . . No, I'm not afraid of him . . .'"

The postmistress, thoroughly enjoying reporting the telephone conversation, pointed a finger at Maigret and declared:

"He meant you, didn't he? . . . So he said he wasn't afraid of you, but that because of Groult-Cotelle who was thoroughly unreliable . . . Ssh . . ."

The bell rang in the post office. The little old lady rushed next door and switched on the light.

"Hello! . . . What? . . . Galvani 17.98? I don't know . . . No, there shouldn't be any delay at this time of night . . . I'll call you back."

Galvani 17.98 was Bréjon's home telephone number and Maigret recognized it at once.

He looked at his watch to see what time it was. Ten minutes to eleven. Unless he had gone to the cinema or the theater with his family, the examining magistrate was bound to be in bed, for everyone at the Palais de Justice knew that he got up at six in the morning and studied his briefs as day broke.

The plugs went into different holes.

"Is that Niort? Can you get me Galvani 17.98? Line 3 is free? Will you connect me, please? Line 2 was awful just now . . . How are you? . . . You're on duty all night? . . . What? . . . No, you know perfectly well I never go to bed before one in the morning . . . Yes, there's fog here too . . . You can't see more than a couple of yards in front of you . . . It'll be icy on the roads tomorrow morning . . . Hello! Paris? . . . Paris? . . . Hello! Paris? . . . Galvani 17.98? . . . Come on, dear . . . Speak more clearly . . . I want Galvani 17.98 . . . What? . . . It's ringing? . . . I can't hear anything . . . Let it go on ringing . . . It's urgent . . . Yes, now there's someone . . ."

She turned around, terrified, for Maigret's bulky frame towered behind her as he stretched out a hand, ready to take the headset at the appropriate moment.

"Monsieur Naud? . . . Hello! . . . Monsieur Naud? . . . Yes, I'm putting you through . . . One moment, it's ringing . . . Hold on . . . Galvani 17.98? Saint-Aubin, here . . . Here's line 3 . . . Go ahead, 3 . . ."

She did not dare protest when the superintendent took the headset authoritatively from her and put it on his head. She put the plug firmly in the hole.

"Hello! Is that you, Victor? . . . What? . . ."

There was interference on the line and Maigret had the feeling that the examining magistrate was taking the call in bed. A moment later, he heard him say for the second time, having heard his brother-in-law's name:

"It's Etienne . . ."

He was probably speaking to his wife who was lying in bed beside him.

"What? . . . There has been a new development? . . .

No? . . . Yes? . . . You're speaking too loudly . . . It's making the line buzz . . ."

For Etienne Naud was one of those men who yell down the telephone as if they are afraid of not being heard.

"Hello! . . . Listen, Victor . . . There's nothing new to report really, no . . . Believe me . . . I'll write to you, anyhow . . . Maybe I'll come and see you in Paris in two or three days' time . . ."

"Please talk more slowly . . . Move over a bit, Marthe . . ."

"What did you say?"

"I was telling Marthe to move over . . . Well? . . . What's going on? The superintendent arrived safely, didn't he? . . . What's your view?"

"Yes . . . Never mind . . . In fact it's because of him that I am calling . . ."

"Doesn't he want to investigate the case?"

"Yes . . . But he's investigating it too thoroughly . . . Listen, Victor, you've simply got to find a way of getting him back to Paris . . . No, I can't talk now . . . I know the postmistress and . . ."

Maigret smiled as he watched the tiny postmistress. She was bubbling over with curiosity.

"You'll find a way, I'm sure . . . What? It will be difficult? . . . But you must be able to, somehow . . . It is absolutely vital. I promise you . . ."

It was not hard to picture the examining magistrate

frowning anxiously as waves of suspicion with regard to
his brother-in-law began to creep into his mind.

"It is not what you are thinking . . . But he's poking
his nose here and there, talking to everyone and doing
far more harm than good . . . Do you see? . . . If he goes
on much longer, the whole town will be in an uproar
and my position will become untenable . . ."

"I don't know what to do . . ."

"Aren't you on good terms with his boss?"

"Yes, I am . . . Of course, I could ask the head of the
Police Judiciaire . . . It's a delicate matter . . . The superintendent will find out sooner or later. It was a pure
favor to me that he agreed to go . . . Do you understand?"

"Do you or don't you want to cause trouble for your
niece? And she's your god-daughter, may I remind
you . . ."

"It really is a serious matter, then?"

"I have already told you . . ."

One had the impression that Etienne Naud was
stamping his feet with impatience. Alban's own panic
had rubbed off on him and the fact that Cavre had not
been against his calling Bréjon to get him to summon
Maigret back to Paris had not exactly reassured him.

"Can I not have a word with my sister?"

"Your sister has gone to bed . . . I'm the only one
downstairs . . ."

"What does Geneviève say?"

The examining magistrate was obviously beginning to falter, and fell back on commonplace remarks.

"Is it raining in your part of the world, too?"

"I don't know!" yelled back Naud. "I don't care a damn! Do you hear? Just get that confounded superintendent of yours out of here . . ."

"What on earth has got into you?"

"What has got into me? If this goes on, we won't be able to stay here, that's all. He is poking his nose into everything. He says nothing. He . . . he . . ."

"Now calm down. I'll do my best."

"When?"

"Tomorrow morning . . . I'll go and see the head of the Police Judiciaire as soon as the offices are open, but it goes against the grain, let me tell you. It's the first time in my career that . . ."

"But you will do it, won't you?"

"I've told you I will . . ."

"The telegram will probably arrive at about noon . . . He'll be able to take the three o'clock train . . . Make sure the telegram arrives in time . . ."

"Is Louise all right?"

"Yes, she's all right . . . Good night . . . Don't forget . . . I'll explain later . . . And don't start imagining things, please . . . Say good night to your wife for me . . ."

The postmistress realized from the look on Maigret's face that the conversation was over and she took the headset from him and moved the plugs once more.

"Hello! . . . Have you finished? . . . Hello, Paris . . . How many calls? . . . Two? . . . Thank you . . . Good night, my dear."

And then she turned to the superintendent, who was putting his hat on again and relighting his pipe:

"I could be sacked for this . . . Do you think it is true, then?"

"What?"

"What people are saying . . . can't think that a man like Monsieur Etienne who has everything he could possibly want to make him happy . . ."

"Good night, mademoiselle. Don't worry. I'll be very discreet . . ."

"What did they say?"

"Nothing much. Just family news . . ."

"Are you going back to Paris?"

"Maybe . . . My goodness, yes . . . It is quite possible I'll take the train tomorrow afternoon . . ."

Maigret was calm, now. He felt himself again. He was almost surprised to find Louis waiting for him in the kitchen and the youngster was equally surprised when he sensed his hero's mood had changed. The superintendent paid virtually no attention to the lad. His attitude towards him was flippant, scornful even, or so thought young Louis who was cut to the quick.

Once more, they began to make their way through the fog which seemed to reduce the world to absurdly small proportions. As before, an occasional light shone through the gloom.

"He did it, didn't he?"

"Who? . . . Did what?"

"Naud . . . He's the one who killed Albert . . ."

"I honestly don't know, my boy . . . It . . ."

Maigret stopped himself in time. He was going to say:

"It doesn't matter . . ."

For that was what he thought, or rather what he felt.
But he realized that a statement such as this would only
startle the youngster.

"What did he say?"

"Nothing much . . . Incidentally, speaking of Groult-
Cotelle . . ."

They were approaching the two inns. The lights
were still on, and on one side of the street faces could be
seen through the window like silhouettes in a Chinese
shadow play.

"Well?"

"Has he always been a close friend of the Nauds?"

"Wait a minute . . . Not always, no . . . I was a small
boy at the time, you see . . . The house has been in his
family for a long time, but when I was a kid we used to
go there to play . . . It was empty then . . . I remember
because we got into the cellar quite a few times . . . One
of the airholes didn't shut properly. Monsieur Groult-
Cotelle was living with some relations of his, then. They
have a castle in Brittany, I think . . . When he came
back here, he was married . . . You should ask some of
the older inhabitants . . . I must have been six or seven
at the time . . . I remember his wife had a lovely little

yellow car which she drove herself and she often used to
go off in it alone . . ."

"Did the two of them visit the Nauds?"

"No . . . I am sure they didn't . . . I say that because I
remember Monsieur Groult was always in a huddle
with the old doctor, a widower . . . I often used to see
them sitting by the window playing chess . . . Unless
I'm mistaken, it was because of his wife he didn't see
the Nauds . . . He was friendly with them before as he
and Naud went to the same school . . . They used to say
hello to each other in the street . . . I used to see them
chatting on the pavement, but that's all . . ."

"So it was after Madame Groult-Cotelle left . . ."

"Yes . . . About three years ago . . . Mademoiselle
Naud was sixteen or seventeen years old . . . She was
back from school—she was at a boarding school in
Niort for a long time and only used to appear every
fourth Sunday . . . I remember that, too, because whenever you saw her during term-time you knew it was
the third Sunday in the month . . . They became
friends . . . Monsieur Groult used to spend half his time
at the Nauds' . . ."

"Do they go off on holiday together?"

"Yes, to Les Sables d'Olonne . . . The Nauds had a
villa built there . . . Are you going back? . . . Don't you
want to know if the detective . . ."

The young lad looked back at Groult-Cotelle's
house and could still see a glimmer of light filtering
through the shutters. Although he dared not show it, he

was somewhat disillusioned with the unorthodox way Maigret seemed to be conducting this inquiry, for he had certainly thought in terms of a very different approach.

"What did he say when you went in?"

"Cavre? Nothing . . . No, he didn't say anything . . . It's not important, anyway . . ."

The fact of the matter was, that at that particular moment, Maigret was living in a world of his own and not in the present at all, and he answered the boy half-heartedly without really knowing what the question was.

Many a time at the Police Judiciaire, his colleagues had joked about his going off into one of these reveries, and he also knew that people used to talk about this habit of his behind his back.

At such moments, Maigret seemed to puff himself up out of all proportion and become slow-witted and stodgy, like someone blind and dumb who is unaware of what is going on around him. Indeed, if anyone not forewarned was to walk past or talk to Maigret when he was in one of these moods, he would more than likely take him for a fat idiot or a fat sleepyhead.

"So, you're concentrating your thoughts?" said someone who prided himself on his psychological perception.

And Maigret had replied with comic sincerity:

"I never think."

And it was almost true. For Maigret was not thinking now, as he stood in the damp, cold street. He was not following through an idea. One might say he was rather like a sponge.

It was Sergeant Lucas who had described him thus, and he had worked constantly with Maigret and knew him better than anyone.

"There comes a time in the course of an investigation," Lucas had said, "when the *patron* suddenly swells up like a sponge. You'd think he was filling up."

But filling up with what? At present, for instance, he was absorbing the fog and the darkness. The village round him was not just any old village. And he was not merely someone who had been cast into these surroundings by chance.

He was rather like God the Father. He knew this village like the back of his hand. It was as if he had always lived here, or better still, as if he had created the little town. He knew what went on inside all those small, low houses nestling in the darkness. He could see men and women turning in the moist warmth of their beds and he followed the thread of their dreams. A dim light in a window enabled him to see a mother, half-asleep, giving a bottle of warm milk to her infant. He felt the shooting pain of the sick woman in the corner and imagined the drowsy grocer's wife waking up with a start.

He was in the café. Men holding grubby cards and totting up red and yellow counters were seated at the brown, polished tables.

He was in Geneviève's bedroom. He was suffering

with her, feeling for her pride as a woman. Doubtless, she had just lived through the most painful day of her life and was perhaps anxiously awaiting Maigret's return so that she could slip into his room once more.

Madame Naud was wide awake. She had gone to bed, but could not get to sleep and in the darkness of her room, she lay listening for the slightest sound in the house. She wondered why Maigret had not come back, pictured her husband cooling his heels in the drawing-room, torn between hope after his telephone call to Bréjon and anxiety at the superintendent's absence.

Maigret felt the warmth of the cattle in the stables, heard the mare kicking, visualized the old cook in her camisole . . . And in Groult-Cotelle's house . . . Look now! A door was opening. Alban was leading his visitor out. How he hated him. What had he and Cavre said to each other in the dusty, stale-smelling sitting room after the telephone call to Naud?

The door closed again. Cavre walked quickly along, his briefcase under his arm. He was pleased, yet displeased. After all, he had almost won the game. He had beaten Maigret. Tomorrow the superintendent would be summoned back to Paris. But none the less, he felt a little humiliated that he had not brought this about single-handed. Furthermore, he felt thoroughly ruffled by the superintendent's menacing tone with regard to the whereabouts of Albert Retailleau's cap . . .

Cavre's employee would be waiting for him at the Lion d'Or, drinking brandy to while away the time.

"Are you going back straightaway?" asked Louis.

"Yes, lad . . . What else can I do?"

"You're not going to give up?"

"Give up what?"

Maigret knew them all so well! He had come across so many lads like Louis in his life, youngsters who were just as enthusiastic, just as naive and crafty, who plunged straight into every difficulty in their desire to solve the case come what may!

"You'll get over it, my lad," he thought. "In a few years' time you will bow respectfully to a Naud or a Groult-Cotelle because you'll have understood that it's the wisest course of action when you're Fillou's son . . ."

And what about Madame Retailleau, all alone in her house? She was sure to have carefully removed all the notes from the soup tureen. She had understood long ago. She had doubtless been as good a wife and as good a mother as anyone else. It was probably not that she lacked feelings, but that she had realized that feelings are of no use. She had resigned herself to this truth.

But she was determined to defend herself with other arms! She was determined to turn all life's misfortunes into banknotes. Her husband's death had secured her her house and an income which allowed her to bring up and educate her son.

The death of Albert . . .

"I bet," he muttered to himself in a low voice, "she wants a little house in Niort, not in Saint-Aubin . . . A brand-new little house, spotlessly clean, with pictures of her husband and son on the wall . . . somewhere she can live comfortably and securely in her old age."

As for Groult-Cotelle and his *Sexual Perversions* . . .

"You're walking awfully quickly, superintendent . . ."

"Are you coming back with me?"

"Do you mind?"

"Won't your mother be worried?"

"Oh! She doesn't take any notice of me . . ."

He said these words with a mixture of pride and regret in his voice.

Off they went, past the station, along the waterlogged path bordering the canal. Old Désiré would be sleeping off his wine on his dirty straw mattress. Josaphat the postman was proud of himself and was no doubt reckoning what he had gained from his cleverness and cunning . . .

Ahead of them, at the end of the path, there was a circle of light like the moon seen through the veil of a cloud. A large, warm and peaceful-looking house pierced the mist, one of those houses that passers-by look at enviously and think how nice it must be to live there.

"Off you go, son . . . We're here now . . ."

"When will I see you again? Promise me you won't leave without . . ."

"I promise . . ."

"You're sure you're not giving up?"

"Sure . . ."

Alas! For Maigret was not exactly thrilled at the

thought of what remained to be done and walked up to the steps of the house with his shoulders down. The front door was ajar. They had left it like this so that he could get in. There was a light on in the drawing-room.

He sighed as he took off his heavy overcoat which the fog had made even heavier, then stood for a moment on the doormat to light his pipe.

"In we go!"

Poor Etienne had sat up waiting for him, torn between hope and a deadly anxiety. That very afternoon, Madame Naud had tormented herself in similar fashion, in the same armchair as her husband was sitting in now.

A bottle of armagnac on a small round table looked as if it had served its purpose well.

8

MAIGRET PLAYS MAIGRET

There was nothing affected about Maigret's stance. If his shoulders were hunched and his head slightly to one side, as if he were frozen to the marrow and bent on warming himself by the stove, it was because he was cold. He had been out in the fog for some time and had paid no attention to the temperature outside. He shivered now as he took off his overcoat and suddenly seemed aware of the icy dampness that chilled his bones.

He felt irritable, as one does when one is about to go down with flu. He also felt uneasy, since he disliked the task which faced him. And he was hesitant. As he was about to go into the drawing room, he suddenly thought of two diametrically opposed methods of tackling the situation, just when he had to make up his mind one way or the other.

It was this, rather than an attempt to live up to his reputation, that made him walk into the room, swerving to and fro like a bear, with a churlish expression on his face and large eyes that did not appear to be focusing on anything.

He looked at nothing, yet saw everything: the glass

and the bottle of armagnac, the smooth hair of Etienne Naud who said with a false cheerfulness:

"Did you have a good evening, superintendent?"

He had obviously just run a comb through his hair. He always kept one in his pocket for he liked to be admired. But before, while he was gloomily waiting for Maigret to come back, he had probably run his shaking fingers through his hair.

Instead of replying, Maigret went over to the wall on the left and adjusted a picture which was not hanging straight. Nor was this affectation. He could not abide seeing a picture hang crooked on a wall. It quite simply irritated him and he had no wish to be irritated for such a stupid reason just when he was all set to play the detective.

It was stuffy. The smell of food still lingered in the room and mingled with the bouquet from the armagnac, to which the superintendent finally helped himself.

"There!" he sighed.

Naud jumped in surprise and anxiety at that resounding "There!" for it was as if Maigret, having debated the situation in his mind, had reached a conclusion.

If the superintendent had been at Police Headquarters or had even been officially investigating the case, he would have felt obliged, in order to make the odds in his favor, to use traditional methods. Now, traditional methods in this case tended to break down Naud's resistance, to scare him and shatter his nerves by making him oscillate between hope and fear.

It was easy. Just let him get entangled in his own lies first. Then vaguely bring up the subject of the two telephone calls. And then (why not, after all?) say point-blank:

"Your friend Alban will be arrested tomorrow morning . . ."

Not a bit of it, however! Maigret quite simply stood with his elbows resting on the mantelpiece. The flames in the fireplace scorched his legs. Naud was sitting near him presumably going on hoping . . .

"I shall leave tomorrow at three o'clock as you wish," sighed the superintendent at last, having puffed at his pipe two or three times in quick succession.

He pitied Naud. He felt uncomfortable before this man who was about the same age as himself and who up until now had lived a comfortable, peaceful, upright life. Now, threatened as he was by the thought of being shut behind prison walls for the rest of his days, he was playing his last cards.

Was he going to carry on the struggle and go on lying? Maigret hoped not, just as, out of compassion, one hopes that a wounded animal, clumsily shot, will die quickly. He avoided looking at him and fixed his eyes on the carpet.

"Why do you say that, superintendent? You know you are welcome here and that my family not only likes but respects you, as I do . . ."

"I overheard your telephone conversation with your brother-in-law, Monsieur Naud."

He put himself in the other man's shoes. Afterwards, he preferred to forget such moments as these. He therefore hurried on:

"Furthermore, you are mistaken about me. Your brother-in-law Bréjon asked me as a favor to come and help you with a delicate matter. I realized straight-away, believe me, that he had wrongly interpreted your wishes and that it was not help of this kind that you wanted from him. You wrote to him in a moment of panic to ask his advice. You told him about the rumors circulating but you did not admit, of course, that they were true. And he, poor man, being an honest, conscientious magistrate who works by the book, sent you a detective to sort out the mess."

Naud struggled slowly to his feet, walked over to the small, round table and poured himself a generous glass of armagnac. His hand was shaking. There were probably beads of sweat on his forehead, although Maigret could not see. No doubt out of consideration for Naud's feelings, the superintendent had looked the other way at this crucial moment, for he pitied the man.

"If you had not called in Justin Cavre, I would have left the district immediately after our initial meeting, but his presence somehow goaded me into staying."

Naud said not a word in protest, but fiddled with his watch chain and stared at the portrait of his mother-in-law.

"Of course, since I am not here on official business, I am not accountable to anyone. So you have nothing to fear from me, Monsieur Naud, and I am in a position to talk to you all the more freely. You have just been through a hellish few weeks, haven't you? And so has your wife, for I am sure she knows all about it . . ."

The other man still did not respond. It had got to the point where a nod of the head, a whisper or a flutter of the eyelids was all that was required to put an end to the suspense. After that, peace would come. He could relax. He would have nothing more to hide, no game to play.

Upstairs, his wife was probably awake, listening carefully and fretting because there was no sign of the two men coming up to bed. And what of his daughter? Had she managed to get to sleep?

"Now, Monsieur Naud, I am going to tell you what I really think, and you will understand why I have not left without saying anything, which strange though it may seem, I was on the point of doing. Listen carefully, and don't be too ready to misconstrue what I say. I have the distinct impression, the near certitude, that however guilty you may be of the death of Albert Retailleau, you are also a victim of his death. I will go further. If you have been the instrument of death, you are not primarily responsible for it."

And Maigret helped himself to a drink, in turn, in order to give the other man time to weigh up his words. As Naud remained silent, he finally looked him in the eye and forced him to look back. He asked:

"Don't you trust me?"

The result was as distressing as it was unexpected,

for Naud, a man in the prime of his life, capitulated by bursting into tears. His swollen eyelids brimmed with tears and he pouted his lips like a child. He fought back the tears for a moment, standing awkwardly in the middle of the room, and then rushed over and leaned against the wall. Burying his face in his arms, he started to sob violently, his shoulders moving jerkily up and down.

There was nothing else to do but wait. Twice, he tried to speak, but it was too soon, for he had not regained sufficient composure. As if out of discretion, Maigret had sat down in front of the fire and, not being able to poke the fire as he was accustomed to doing in his own home, he arranged the logs with a pair of tongs.

"You can tell me in your own words what happened in a little while, if you like, although it won't serve much purpose as it is a simple matter to reconstruct the events of the night in question. But what followed is another matter altogether . . ."

"What do you mean?"

Naud looked just as tall and strong, but he seemed to have lost his grip. He had the air of a child who has shot up too quickly and who at the age of twelve is as tall and well-filled out as a fully grown man.

"Did you not suspect there was something going on between your daughter and that young man?"

"But I didn't even know him, superintendent! I mean I knew of his existence because I know more or less everyone in the village, but I could not have put a name to his face. I still wonder how on earth Geneviève managed to meet him as she virtually never left the house . . ."

"On the night in question, you and your wife were in bed, were you not?"

"Yes . . . And another thing . . . It's ridiculous, but we'd had goose for dinner . . ."

He clung to facts of this kind, as though investing the truth with such intimate details somehow made it less tragic.

"I love goose, but I find it difficult to digest . . . At about one in the morning, I got up to take some bicarbonate of soda . . . You know the layout of the rooms upstairs, more or less . . . Our bathroom is next to our bedroom, then there's a spare room and next to that a room we never go into because . . ."

"I know . . . In memory of a child . . ."

"My daughter's room is at the far end of the corridor and so it is rather isolated from the rest of the house. The two maids sleep on the floor above . . . So I was in our bathroom groping about in the dark, as I didn't want to wake up my wife, as she'd have scolded me for being greedy . . . I heard the sound of voices . . . There was an argument going on . . . It did not cross my mind that the noise could be coming from my daughter's room . . .

"However, when I went into the corridor to see for myself, I realized this was so. There was a light beneath her door, too . . . I heard a man's voice . . .

"I don't know what you would have done in my

place, superintendent . . . I don't know if you have a daughter . . . We're still rather behind the times here in Saint-Aubin . . . Perhaps I am particularly naive . . . Geneviève is twenty . . . But it had never occurred to me she might hide something like this from her mother and me . . . To think that a man . . . No! You know, even now . . ."

He wiped his eyes and mechanically took his packet of cigarettes out of his pocket.

"I almost rushed into the room in my night-shirt . . . I'm rather old-fashioned in that respect, too, as I still wear nightshirts and not pajamas . . . But at the last moment I realized how ridiculous I looked and went back into the bathroom. I got dressed in the dark and just as I was putting on my socks, I heard another noise, this time from outside . . . As the bathroom shutters had not been closed I drew back the curtain . . . There was a moon and I could see a man climbing down a ladder into the courtyard . . .

"I got my shoes on somehow . . . I rushed down-stairs . . . I am not sure, but I think I heard my wife calling:

"'Etienne . . .'

"Have you already thought of looking at the key to the door which opens on to the courtyard? . . . It's an old key, a huge one, a real hammer . . . I would not be prepared to swear I took it off its hook without thinking, but it wasn't a premeditated action either for it had not occurred to me to kill and if anyone had said then . . ."

He spoke softly but in a shaky voice. To calm himself down he lit his cigarette and puffed slowly at it several times, like condemned men must do.

"The man went around the house and jumped over the low wall by the road. I jumped over it behind him, not thinking to stifle the sound of my footsteps. He must have heard me but he went on walking at the same pace. When I had almost caught up with him he turned around, and although I could not see his face, for some reason or other I got the impression he was jeering at me.

"'What do you want of me?' he asked in an aggressive, scornful tone of voice.

"I swear to you, superintendent, there are moments I wish with all my heart I had never lived through. I recognized him. He was just a youngster to me, but he had just left my daughter's bedroom and now he was sneering at me. I didn't know what to do. This kind of thing doesn't happen the way you imagine. I shook him by the shoulders but couldn't find the words to express what I wanted to say.

"'So you're annoyed I am jilting your daughter, are you! The slut! . . . You were hand in glove, weren't you?' he flung at me."

Naud passed his hand over his face.

"I am not sure of anything, any more, superintendent. With the best will in the world, I could not give you an exact account of what happened. He was every bit as angry as I was but more in control of himself. He was insulting me, insulting my daughter . . . Instead of falling on his knees at my feet, as I had stupidly half-imagined he would do, he was making fun of me, my wife, my whole family. He said things like:

"'A fine family, indeed!'

"He used the most obscene language when referring to my daughter, words I cannot bring myself to repeat, and then I began to hit him. I don't know how it happened. I had the key in my hand. The youth suddenly punched me hard in the stomach and the pain was such that I hit him more violently than ever . . .

"He fell . . .

"And then I ran away. All I wanted to do was to get back to the house . . .

"I swear to you this is the truth . . . My idea was to telephone the gendarmerie in Benet . . . When I got closer to the house I saw a light on in my daughter's room . . . I suddenly thought that if I told the truth . . . But you must understand . . . I went back to where I had left him . . . He was dead . . ."

"You carried him to the railway line," Maigret interceded, to help him bring this sorry story more quickly to an end.

"That's right . . ."

"All by yourself?"

"Yes . . ."

"And you returned home?"

"My wife was standing behind the door that opens on to the road. She asked in a whisper:

"'What have you done?'

"I tried to deny it all, but she knew. There was terror and pity in the look she gave me. I went to bed feeling somewhat feverish and she went through my clothes in turn in the bathroom to make sure that . . ."

"I understand."

"You may or may not believe it, but neither my wife nor I have had the courage to broach the subject with our daughter. We've never talked about it or even re-ferred to it together. That's probably the hardest thing of all. It is sometimes unnerving. Our household routine is exactly the same as it was in the past and yet all three of us know . . ."

"And Alban?"

"I don't know how to tell you. At first, I did not give him a thought. Then the next day I was surprised he didn't turn up as usual as we were about to eat. I started to talk about him for the sake of something to say . . . I said: 'I must give Alban a call.'

"I did so, and his maid told me he wasn't in . . . However, I was certain I heard his voice when the maid answered the phone . . .

"It became an obsession with me . . . Why doesn't Alban come? Does Alban suspect something? . . . Stupid as it may seem, I convinced myself that he constituted the only real threat, and four days later, when he still hadn't looked in on us, I went over to his house.

"I wanted to know the reason for his silence. I had no intention of confiding in him, but somehow I ended up telling him everything . . .

"I needed him . . . You would understand why if you had been in my position. He used to tell me the local gossip . . . He also described the funeral.

"I was well aware of what people were thinking from the outset and another idea took root in my mind. I felt I had to atone for what I had done and this thought never left me . . . Don't laugh at me, I beg of you . . ."

"I have seen so many men like you, Monsieur Naud!"

"And did they behave as stupidly as I did? Did they, one fine day, go and see the victim's mother like I did? In melodramatic fashion, I waited until it was dark one evening, and then paid her a visit after Groult had made sure there was no one on the road . . . I did not tell her the brutal truth . . . I said that it was a terrible misfortune to have befallen her, that as a widow she had lost her only source of support . . .

"I am not sure whether it was a devil or an angel that prompted me, superintendent. I can still see her, white-faced and motionless, standing by the hearth with a shawl round her shoulders. I had twenty 1000 franc notes in two bundles in my pocket. I didn't know how to go about putting them on the table. I was ashamed of myself. I was . . . yes, I was ashamed of her too . . .

"And yet the notes passed from my pocket to the table.

"'Each year, madame, I will make it my duty to . . .'

"And as she frowned, I hurriedly added: 'Unless you would rather I give you a lump sum in your name which . . .'"

He could not go on and had such difficulty in breathing that he had to pour himself another glass of armagnac.

"There it is . . . I was wrong not to confess to everything at the beginning . . . It was too late afterwards . . . Nothing had changed at home, at least superficially . . . I don't know how Geneviève has had the courage to go on living as if nothing had happened. There have been times when I have wondered if my imagination hasn't been playing tricks on me . . .

"When I realized that people in the village suspected me, when I began receiving anonymous letters and found out that more had been sent to the Department of Public Prosecutions, I wrote to my brother-in-law. It was stupid of me, for what could he do as I had not told him the truth? One so often hears it said that magistrates have the power to cover up a scandal that I vaguely imagined Bréjon would use his authority in the same way . . .

"Instead, however, he sent you down here just when I had written to a private detective agency in Paris . . . Yes! I did that too! I picked an address at random from the newspaper advertisements! Unable to bring myself to confide in my brother-in-law, I told a total stranger everything that had happened. I simply had to be reassured . . .

"He knew you were on your way, for when my brother-in-law told me you were arriving I immediately sent a telegram to Cavre's agency ... We arranged to meet in Fontenay the following day ...

"What else do you want to know, superintendent? ... How you must despise me! ... Yes, you do! ... And I despise myself too, I assure you ... Of all the criminals you have known, I bet you haven't come across one as stupid, as ..."

Maigret smiled for the first time. Etienne Naud was sincere. There was nothing artificial about his despair. And yet, as with all criminals, to use the word he himself had just used, his attitude revealed a certain pride.

It was annoying and humiliating to have bungled being a criminal!

For a few seconds, or even a few minutes, Maigret sat quite still and stared down at the flames curling round the blackened logs. Etienne Naud was so disconcerted by this unexpected reaction on the part of the superintendent that he was at a loss what to do and stood hesitantly in the middle of the room, unsure of his next move.

The fact of the matter was, that since he had confessed to everything, since he had chosen to abase himself, he had naturally supposed that the superintendent would show him more consideration and come morally to his assistance.

Had he not sunk lower than the low? Had he not painted a pathetic picture of his own and his family's plight?

Earlier on, before confessing, Naud had sensed that Maigret was already sympathetic to his case and prepared to be more so. He had counted on this.

And now, all trace of sympathy had vanished. The game was over and the superintendent was calmly smoking his pipe, his expression one of deep thought devoid of any sentimentality.

"What would you do in my position?" ventured Naud once more.

One look made him wonder if he had gone too far. Perhaps he had overstepped the mark like a child who is forgiven for misbehaving and as a result of such lenient treatment becomes more demanding and tiresome than ever.

What was Maigret thinking? Naud began to suspect that his manner had merely been part of a trap. He expected him to rise to his feet, take a pair of handcuffs out of his pocket and say the sacred words:

"In the name of the law . . ."

"I am wondering . . ."

It was Maigret who hesitated, still puffing at his pipe as he crossed and uncrossed his legs.

"I am wondering . . . yes . . . I am wondering if we couldn't telephone your friend, Alban . . . What time is it? . . . Ten minutes past midnight . . . The postmistress will probably still be up and will put us through . . . Yes, indeed . . . If you're not too tired, Monsieur Naud, I think it would be best if we got everything over with tonight so that I can catch my train tomorrow . . ."

"But . . ."

He could not find the right words, or rather dared not say what was on the tip of his tongue:

"But isn't it all over?"

"Will you excuse me?"

Maigret walked across the drawing-room into the hall and turned the handle of the telephone.

"Hello . . . I am sorry to bother you, dear mademoiselle . . . Yes, it's me . . . Did you recognize my voice? . . . Of course not . . . No problem at all . . . Could you very kindly put me through to Monsieur Groult-Cotelle, please? . . . Let it ring loud and clear in case he's a heavy sleeper."

Through the half-open door, he saw a bewildered Etienne Naud take a large gulp of armagnac, as though resigned to his fate. The poor man was in a terrible state and seemed to have lost all his strength and nerve.

"Monsieur Groult-Cotelle? . . . How are you? . . . You had gone to bed . . . What's that? . . . You were reading in bed? . . . Yes, Superintendent Maigret here . . . Yes, I'm with your friend . . . We've been having a chat . . . What? . . . You've got a cold? . . . That's most unfortunate . . . Anyone would think you have guessed what I was going to say . . . We would like you to pop over here . . . Yes, I know it is foggy . . . You haven't any clothes on? . . . Well, in that case we'll come to you . . . We'll be round in a jiffy if we take the car . . . What? . . . You'd rather come over here? . . .

No . . . Nothing in particular . . . I am leaving tomorrow . . . I have important business to see to in Paris . . ."

Poor Naud understood less and less what was in Maigret's mind and stared up at the ceiling, thinking to himself no doubt that his wife could hear everything and must be thoroughly alarmed. Should he go upstairs to reassure her? But was he really in a position to do so? Maigret's behavior now made him uneasy and he was beginning to regret having admitted to the crime.

"What did you say? . . . A quarter of an hour? . . . That's too long . . . Be as quick as you can . . . See you in a minute . . . Thank you . . ."

Perhaps the superintendent was play-acting to a certain extent. Perhaps he was not really angry? Perhaps he did not want to be alone with Etienne Naud and have to wait ten minutes or a quarter of an hour in the drawing room with him?

"He is coming over," he announced. "He's very worried. You cannot imagine what a state my telephone call has put him in . . ."

"But he's got no reason to . . ."

"Is that what you think?" asked Maigret simply.

Naud was more and more perplexed.

"Do you mind if I go and get a bite to eat in the kitchen . . . Stay where you are . . . I'll find the light switch . . . I know where the fridge is . . ."

He switched on the light in the kitchen. The stove

had gone out. He found a chicken leg glazed with sauce. He cut and buttered a thick slice of bread.

"Tell me . . ."

He came back into the drawing room smiling.

"Have you got any beer?"

"Wouldn't you rather have a glass of Burgundy?"

"I'd prefer beer, but if you haven't got any . . ."

"There must be some in the cellar . . . I always have one or two crates brought in but as we don't drink beer very often, I don't know if . . ."

Just as, during the saddest of deathbed scenes, the family will cease weeping for a moment in the middle of the night and have a little something to eat, so the two men, after an hour of high drama, went matter-of-factly down to the cellar.

"No . . . This is lemonade . . . Wait a minute . . . The beer must be underneath the stairs . . ."

He was right. They went back upstairs with bottles of beer under their arms and then set about finding two large glasses. Maigret went on munching the chicken leg which he held between his fingers and got the sauce all over his chin.

"I wonder," he said casually, "if your friend Alban will come alone."

"What do you mean?"

"Nothing. I'm willing to bet that . . ."

There was no time to finish the wager, for someone was tapping on the front door. Etienne Naud rushed to open it. Maigret meanwhile stood calmly waiting in the middle of the drawing room with his glass of beer in one hand and the chicken and bread in the other.

He heard low voices:

"I have taken the liberty of bringing this gentleman with me. I met him on the way over here and he . . ."

For a second, Maigret's eyes hardened and then, with no warning, they suddenly flickered mischievously as he shouted to the man outside:

"Come in, Cavre! I was expecting you . . ."

9

NOISE BEHIND THE DOOR

An impression of a dream can remain within us for a long time, sometimes all our lives, whereas the dream itself, so we are told, only lasts a few seconds. Thus, for a moment, the three men entering the room seemed to Maigret to bear no resemblance to the kind of men they actually were, or at any rate considered themselves to be, and it was this new image of them that was to remain so vividly in his mind in the years to come.

They were all more or less the same age, Maigret included. And as he observed them each in turn he felt rather as if he was looking on at a gathering of school-boys in their last year.

Etienne Naud was probably just as plump and podgy when he took his *bachot* as he was now. He would have had the same sturdy physique, the same soft look about him, and would undoubtedly have been very well-brought-up and rather shy.

The superintendent had met Cavre not long after he had left school and even then he had been a loner, and an ill-tempered one at that. However hard he tried—for he took a pride in his appearance then—clothes simply did not sit as well on him as on other people. He always looked shabby and badly dressed. He was a sad figure. When he was a little boy his mother must have been forever saying to him:

"Run along and play with the others, Justin."

And no doubt she would confide to her neighbors:

"My son never plays. It worries me a bit from the health point of view. He's too clever. He never stops thinking . . ."

As for Alban, his looks had changed remarkably little since he was a young man: the long, thin legs, the elongated, rather aristocratic-looking face, the long, pale hands covered with reddish hairs, the upper-class elegance . . . He would have copied his friends' compositions, borrowed cigarettes from them and told them dirty jokes in corners!

And now they were struggling with utmost seriousness over an affair which could send one of them to jail for life. They were mature men. Two children somewhere bore the name of Groult-Cotelle, children who had perhaps already inherited some of their father's vices. In the house were a wife and daughter who would probably not sleep that night. As for Cavre, he was doubtless fuming at the thought his wife might be making the most of his absence.

Something rather curious was happening. Whereas, shortly before, Etienne had confessed his crime to Maigret without a trace of shame and had laid bare, man to man, his innermost fears, now he blushed to the very roots of his hair as he ushered the visitors into the drawing room, trying in vain to look unconcerned.

Was it not, in fact, rather a childish fancy that caused him to blush so violently? For a few seconds, Maigret became the headmaster or teacher. Naud had remained behind with him to be questioned about some misdeed and be given a wigging. His friends were now coming back into the classroom and looking at him searchingly as if to say:

"How did you get on?"

Well, he had not got on at all well. He had not defended himself. He had wept. He wondered if there were still traces of tears on his cheeks and eyelids.

He would like to have boasted and made them think that everything had gone smoothly. Instead, he bustled about, went into the dining room to get some glasses out of the sideboard and then poured out the armagnac.

Did these glimpses of a time of life when our actions and conduct are as yet unimportant inspire the superintendent? He waited until everyone was seated, then positioned himself in the middle of the room and, looking at Cavre and Alban in turn, said squarely:

"Well, gentlemen, the game's up!"

Only at this point, and for the first time since he had become involved in this case, did he play Maigret, as was said of inspectors at the Police Judiciaire who tried to imitate the great man. With his pipe between his teeth, his hands in his pockets and his back to the fire, he talked, growled, poked at the logs with the end of the tongs and moved with a bearlike gait from one suspect to the other, either firing questions at them or suddenly breaking off so that a disturbing silence fell over the room.

"Monsieur Naud and I have just had a long and friendly chat. I announced my intention of returning to Paris tomorrow. It was far better, was it not, before taking leave of each other, to come out with the truth, and this is what we did. Why do you jump, Monsieur Groult-Cotelle? In fact, Cavre, I must apologize for having made you come out just when you were going to bed. Yes indeed! I am the guilty one. I knew perfectly well when I rang our friend Alban that he wouldn't have the guts to come here alone. I wonder why he considered my invitation to come round for a chat a threat . . . He had a detective to hand and as there was no lawyer around, he brought along the detective . . . Isn't that right, Groult?"

"It wasn't me who sent to Paris for him!" replied the bogus country gentleman, now stripped of his importance.

"I know. It wasn't you who beat the unfortunate Retailleau to death, as you just happened to be in La Roche for the night. It wasn't you who left your wife as she was the one who left you . . . It wasn't you who . . . In fact you're a somewhat negative character altogether, aren't you . . . You have never done a good deed in your life . . ."

Alarmed at being reprimanded like this, Groult-

Cotelle called Cavre to his aid, but the detective, his leather briefcase on his lap, was looking at Maigret in a somewhat anxious fashion.

He was sufficiently well-acquainted with the police, and with the *patron* in particular, to know that this little scene was being staged for a definite purpose and that when the meeting was over, the case would be closed.

Etienne Naud had not protested when the superintendent had declared:

"The game's up!"

What more did Maigret want? He walked up and down, stood in front of one of the portraits, went from one door to the other, all the time keeping up a steady flow of words. It was almost as if he were improvising and now and again Cavre began to wonder if he might not be playing for time and waiting for something to happen which he knew would happen but was taking a long time to do so.

"I am leaving tomorrow, then, as you all wish me to do, and while I am about it, I could reproach you, especially you, Cavre, as you know me, for not having had more confidence in me. You knew quite well, damn it, that I was just a guest and treated as well as ever a guest could be.

"What happened in this house before I arrived does not concern me. At most you could have asked my advice. After all, what is Naud's position? He did something most unfortunate, very unfortunate, even. But did anyone come forward and complain?

"No! The young man's mother declares herself satisfied. If I may say so . . ."

And Maigret deliberately made light of his next,
ominous statement, a tactic which misled all three men.

"The drama in question was enacted by gentlemen,
all well-bred people. There were rumors abroad, admittedly. Two or three unpleasant pieces of evidence gave
cause for concern but the diplomacy of our friend Cavre
and Naud's money, combined with the liking of certain
individuals for liquor, averted any possible danger. And
as for the cap, which in any case would not have constituted sufficient proof, I presume Cavre took the precau-
tion of destroying it. Isn't that right, Justin?"

Cavre jumped on hearing himself addressed by his
Christian name. Everybody turned to look at him but
he said nothing.

"That, in a nutshell, is the position at present, or
rather our host's position. Anonymous letters are in
circulation. The Director of Prosecutions and the gendarmerie have received some of them. There may be an
official inquiry into the case. What have you advised
your client, Cavre?"

"I am not a barrister."

"How modest you are! If you want to know what I
think, and this is my own personal view and not a professional opinion, for I am not a barrister either, in a few
days' time, Naud will feel the need to depart with his
family. He is rich enough to sell his estate and retire
elsewhere, possibly abroad . . ."

Naud let out a sigh in the form of a sob at the thought of leaving what had been his whole life up until now.

"That leaves our friend Alban . . . What do you propose to do, Monsieur Alban Groult-Cotelle?"

"You don't have to answer," Cavre hurriedly interjected on seeing him open his mouth. "I would also like to say that we are under no obligation to put up with this interrogation, which in any case is phoney. If you knew the superintendent as well as I do, you would realize he is taking us for a real ride, as they would say at the Quai des Orfèvres. I don't know whether you have confessed, Monsieur Naud, or how the superintendent got the truth out of you, but of one thing I am sure, and that is that my former colleague has a purpose in mind. I do not know what that purpose is, but I am telling you to be on your guard."

"Well said, Justin!"

"I did not ask for your opinion."

"Well, I am giving it all the same."

And suddenly his tone changed. For the past quarter of an hour he had been waiting for something and had been forced into all this play-acting as a result, but now that something had finally happened. It was not without good reason that he had kept on pacing up and down, going from the hall door to the door opening into the dining room.

Nor was it hunger or greed earlier on that had caused him to go into the kitchen for some bread and a hunk of chicken. He needed to know if there was another staircase besides the one leading down into the hall. And indeed there was a second staircase for the staff near the kitchen.

When he telephoned Groult-Cotelle he had talked in a very loud voice, as though unaware of the fact that two women were supposed to be sleeping in the house.

Now, there was someone behind the half-open dining-room door.

"You are right, Cavre. You are no fool, even though you are rather a sad character . . . I have one purpose in mind and that is, let me declare it immediately, to prove that Naud is not the real culprit . . ."

This statement by the superintendent stupefied Etienne Naud more than anyone else, for he had to restrain himself from crying out. As for Alban, he had turned deadly pale and small red blotches which Maigret had not noticed before appeared on his forehead, as if he were prey to a sudden attack of urticaria—a clear proof of his inner collapse.

When he saw the rash, the superintendent remembered how a certain, more or less notorious murderer, after a twenty-eight-hour interrogation during which he had defended himself step-by-step, had suddenly wet his pants like a frightened child. Maigret and Lucas had been conducting the interrogation and they had sniffed, looked at each other and realized they had the upper hand.

Alban Groult-Cotelle's nettle-rash was a similar symptom of guilt and the superintendent had difficulty in suppressing a smile.

"Tell me, Monsieur Groult, would you rather tell us the truth yourself, or would you like me to do it for you? Take your time before answering. Naturally, you have my permission to consult your lawyer . . . I mean Justin Cavre. Go off into a corner, if you like, and work something out between you . . ."

"I have nothing to say . . ."

"So it is my job to tell Monsieur Naud, who still does not know, why Albert Retailleau was killed, is it? For, strange as it might seem, even though Etienne Naud knows the young man was killed, he has absolutely no idea *why* . . . What were you going to say, Alban?"

"You're a liar!"

"How can you say I am a liar when I haven't said anything yet? Come now! I will put the question a different way and it will still come to the same thing. Will you tell us why, on a certain, carefully chosen day, you suddenly felt the need to go to La Roche-sur-Yon and bring back your hotel bill with meticulous care?"

Etienne Naud still did not understand and looked anxiously at Maigret, convinced that this line of attack would prove the superintendent's undoing. At first he had been impressed by Maigret's manner but now he was rapidly going down in Naud's estimation. His animosity towards Groult-Cotelle was pointless and beginning to be thoroughly obnoxious.

It had reached the point when Naud felt he had to intervene. He was an honest fellow who disliked seeing an innocent man accused, and as host of the house, he would not allow one of his guests to be hauled over the coals.

"I assure you, superintendent, you are barking up the wrong tree . . ."

"My dear fellow, I am sorry to have to disillusion you, and even sorrier that what you are about to learn is extremely unpleasant. Isn't that so, Groult?"

Groult-Cotelle had shot to his feet and for a moment looked as if he was going to rush at his tormentor. He had the greatest possible difficulty in restraining himself. He clenched his fists and his whole body quivered. Finally, he made as if for the door, but Maigret stopped him in his tracks by simply asking in the most natural tone:

"Are you going upstairs?"

Who would have thought, on seeing the stubborn and stolid Maigret, that he was as warm as his victim? His shirt was sticking to his back. He was listening carefully. And the truth of the matter was, he was frightened.

A few minutes before, he'd become convinced that Geneviève was behind the door, as he hoped. He had been thinking of her when he had telephoned Groult-Cotelle earlier on and had consequently talked in a loud voice in the hall.

"If I am right," he was thinking then, "she'll come down . . ."

And she had come down. At all events, he had heard a faint rustling sound behind the double doors into the dining room and one side of them had moved.

It was on Geneviève's account, too, that he had addressed Groult-Cotelle in such a way a moment ago. Now he was wondering if she was still there, for he could not hear a sound. It had crossed his mind that she might have fainted, but presumably he would have heard her fall.

He was longing to look behind the half-open door and began thinking of how he could do so.

"Are you going upstairs?" he had flung at Alban.

And Alban, who seemed no longer to care, retraced his steps and positioned himself a few inches away from his enemy.

"Just what are you insinuating? Out with it! What other slanders have you got up your sleeve? There's not a word of truth in what you are going to say, do you hear?"

"Take a look at your lawyer."

Cavre looked pitiful, indeed, for he realized that Maigret was on the right track and that his client was caught in his own web of lies.

"I don't need anyone to advise me. I don't know what you might have been told or who could have fabricated such stories, but before you say anything, I would like to state that they are untrue. If a few bright sparks have succeeded in . . ."

"You are vile, Groult."

"What?"

"I say that you are a repugnant character. I say and I repeat that you are the real cause of Albert Retailleau's death, and that if the laws created by men were perfect, life imprisonment would not be a harsh enough punishment for you. In fact it would give me great personal pleasure, though I don't often feel like this, to accompany you to the foot of the guillotine . . ."

"Gentlemen, I call you to witness . . ."

"Not only did you kill Retailleau, but others too . . ."

"I killed Retailleau? . . . I? . . . You're mad, superintendent! . . . He's mad! . . . He's stark-raving mad, I swear to you! . . . Where are these people I've killed? . . . Show them to me, then, if you please . . . Well, we're waiting, Monsieur Sherlock Holmes . . ."

He was sneering. His agitation had reached its peak.

"There is one of them . . ." Maigret calmly replied, pointing to Etienne Naud, who was looking increasingly bewildered.

"It seems to me he's a dead man in very good health, as the saying goes, and if all my victims . . ."

Alban had moved closer to Maigret in such an arrogant manner that the superintendent's hand automatically jerked up and came down on Alban's pale cheek with a thud.

Perhaps they were going to come to blows, grip each other by the waist and roll about on the carpet as befitted the schoolboys the superintendent had visualized a short while before. But the sound of a hysterical voice shrieking from the top of the stairs stopped them in their tracks.

"Etienne! . . . Etienne! . . . Superintendent! . . . Quick! . . . Geneviève . . ."

Madame Naud came down a few more steps, amazed no one appeared to have heard her, for she had already been shouting for a good few seconds.

"Hurry . . ." Maigret said to Naud. "Go up to your daughter . . ."

And he turned to face Cavre and said in a tone which invited no reply:

"Just make sure he doesn't escape . . . Do you hear?"

He followed Etienne Naud up the stairs and went with him into the young girl's bedroom.

"Look . . ." moaned Madame Naud, distraught.

Geneviève was lying across her bed with her clothes on. Her eyes were half-open but had the glazed look of a sleepwalker. A phial of veronal lay broken on the carpet where she had dropped it.

"Help me, madame . . ."

The opiate was only now beginning to take effect and the young girl was still half-conscious. She drew back, terrified, as the superintendent bent down and, gripping her hard, forced open her mouth.

"Bring me some water, a lot of water, warm if possible . . ."

"You go, Etienne . . . In the boiler . . ."

Poor Etienne bumped his way down the corridor and backstairs like a giddy goose.

"Don't be afraid, madame . . . We are acting in time . . . It's my fault . . . I didn't think she would react like this . . . Get me a handkerchief, a towel, anything will do . . ."

Less than two minutes later, the young girl had vomited violently. She sat dejectedly on the edge of her bed obediently drinking down all the water the superintendent gave her, which made her sick all over again.

"You can telephone the doctor. He won't do much more, but to be on the safe side . . ."

Geneviève suddenly broke down and began to cry, softly, but with such weariness that the tears seemed to lull her to sleep.

"I'll leave you to look after her, madame . . . I think it is best if she rests before the doctor comes . . . In my opinion—and unfortunately I've seen rather a lot of cases like this, believe me—the danger is over . . ."

They could hear Naud on the telephone downstairs:

"Immediately, yes . . . It's my daughter . . . I'll explain when you get here . . . No . . . Come as you are, in your dressing-gown if you like, it doesn't matter . . ."

As he passed Naud in the hall, Maigret took the letter he was holding in his hand. He had noticed it lying on Geneviève's bedside table but had not had a moment to pick it up.

Naud tried to get the letter back as soon as he had put down the receiver.

"What are you doing?" he exclaimed in astonishment. "It's for her mother and me . . ."

"I will give it back to you in a moment . . . Go upstairs and sit with her . . ."

"But . . ."

"It's the best place for you to be, I promise you."

And Maigret went back into the drawing-room, care-fully closing the door behind him. He held the letter in his hand and was obviously reluctant to open it.

"Well? Groult?"

"You have no right to arrest me."

"I know . . ."

"I have done nothing illegal . . ."

This momentous word almost made Maigret think he deserved to be slapped again, but he would have had to cross the room to do so and he did not feel up to it.

He toyed with the letter and hesitated before finally slitting open the mauve envelope.

"Is that letter addressed to you?" protested Groult-Cotelle.

"No, and it's not addressed to you either . . . Geneviève wrote it before taking the overdose . . . Would you like me to return it to her parents?"

Dear Mommy, dear Daddy,
I love you dearly. I beg you to believe me. But I must put an end to my life. I cannot go on living any longer. Do not try to find out why, and above all, don't ask Alban to the house any more. He . . .

"Tell me, Cavre, did he tell you the whole story while we were upstairs?"

Maigret was convinced that in his agitated state,

Alban had confessed because of a desperate need to cling to someone, a man who could defend him, whose job it was to do so provided he was paid for his services.

As Cavre lowered his head, Maigret added:

"Well, what have you got to say?"

And Groult-Cotelle, whose cowardice knew no limits, chipped in:

"She began it . . ."

"And she, no doubt, gave you nasty little pornographic books to read?"

"I never gave her any . . ."

"And you never showed her certain pictures I saw in your library?"

"She came across them when my back was turned . . ."

"And no doubt you felt the need to explain them to her?"

"I am not the first man of my age to take a young girl for a mistress . . . I didn't force her . . . She was very much in love . . ."

Maigret laughed abusively as he looked Alban up and down.

"And it was her idea, too, to call in Retailleau?"

"If she took another lover, that is certainly no affair of mine, you must admit. I think you have got an absolute nerve to blame me! Me! In front of my friend Naud, just now . . ."

"What was that?"

"In front of Naud, then. I didn't dare answer and you had the upper hand . . ."

A car pulled up in front of the steps. Maigret went out of the room to open the front door and said, just as if he were master of the house:

"Go straight up to Geneviève's room. Hurry . . ."

Then he went back into the drawing-room, still holding Geneviève's letter in his hand.

"It was you, Groult, who panicked when she told you she was pregnant. You're a coward and always have been. You are so afraid of life that you dare not live by your own effort and so you clutch at other people's lives . . .

"He was going to foist that child on some poor idiot who would then become its father . . .

"It was such a practical solution! . . . Geneviève was to ensnare a young man who would think he was sincerely loved . . . He would be told one fine day that his ardor had resulted in a pregnancy . . . He only had to go to her father, ask to be forgiven on bended knees and declare himself willing to make amends . . .

"And you would have gone on being her lover, wouldn't you! You bastard!"

It was young Louis who had put him on the trail when he had said:

"Albert was angry . . . He had several brandies before going off to meet her . . ."

And Albert's behavior toward Geneviève's father? He had been insolent. He had used the most foul language when speaking of Geneviève.

"How did he find out?" demanded Maigret.

"I don't know."

"Would you rather I go and ask Geneviève?"

Groult-Cotelle shrugged his shoulders. What difference did it make, after all? Maigret could not pin a charge on him.

"Every morning Retailleau used to go to the post office to collect his employers' post as it was being sorted . . . He would go behind the counter and sometimes helped to sort the letters . . . He recognized Geneviève's handwriting on an envelope which was addressed to me. She had not been able to see me alone for several days and so . . ."

"I see . . ."

"If that hadn't happened, everything would have gone according to plan . . . And if you hadn't meddled . . ."

Of course Albert had been angry that night, when for the last time he went to see the girl who had used him so shamefully with the incriminating letter in his pocket! Moreover, everyone had conspired to make a fool of him, her parents included, why should he think otherwise?

He had been led a fine dance, and they were still deceiving him. The father was even pretending to have caught him in the act in order to make him marry his daughter . . .

"How did you know he had intercepted the letter?"

"I went to the post office shortly afterwards . . . The postmistress said: 'Wait a minute! I thought there was a letter for you . . .'

"She hunted high and low . . . I rang Geneviève . . . I

asked the postmistress who had been there when they
were sorting the post and then I realized, I . . ."

"You realized that things had taken a turn for the
worse and you decided to go and see your friend, the
préfet's private secretary, in La Roche . . ."

"That's my affair . . ."

"What do you think, Justin?"

But Cavre put off replying. Heavy footsteps were
heard on the stairs. The door opened. Etienne Naud
came in looking downcast and dejected, his large eyes
full of questions he sought in vain to answer. At that
very moment, Maigret dropped the letter he was holding in his hand in so clumsy a fashion that it fell on top
of the logs and flared up immediately.

"What have you done?"

"I'm so sorry . . . It doesn't really matter, as your
daughter is saved and she will be able to tell you herself
what she put in her letter . . ."

Was Naud taken in? Or was his attitude the same as
that of certain patients who suspect they are not being
told the truth, who only half-believe or don't believe at
all the doctor's optimistic words, but who none the less
long to hear these very words and so be reassured at
whatever price?

"She is much better now, isn't she?"

"She is asleep . . . The danger is over, it seems, thanks
to your swift action . . . I thank you from the bottom of
my heart, superintendent . . ."

The poor fellow seemed to be swimming about in the drawing room, as if it had suddenly become too large for him, like an article of clothing that has stretched and swamps the wearer. He looked at the bottle of armagnac, almost poured himself a glass, but a sense of modesty held him back and in the end Maigret had to do it for him. He helped himself to a glass at the same time.

"Here's to your daughter and the end of all these misunderstandings . . ."

Naud looked up at him in wide-eyed astonishment, for "misunderstanding" was the very last word he had expected to hear.

"We have been chatting while you were upstairs . . . I think your friend Groult has something very important to say to you . . . Believe it or not, he is in the process of getting a divorce, though he hasn't told a soul . . ."

Naud looked more and more at sea.

"Yes . . . And he has other plans . . . All this probably won't make you jump for joy . . . Two wrongs don't make a right, I know, but it's a start, anyway . . . Well! I'm asleep on my feet . . . Didn't someone say just now there was a morning train?"

"It leaves at 6:11," said Cavre. "I think I'll take it, what's more . . ."

"We'll travel together, then . . . and in the meantime, I am going to try and snatch a few hours' sleep . . ."

He could not help saying to Alban as he went out:

"What a dirty trick!"

It was still foggy. Maigret point-blank refused to let anyone take him to the station and Etienne Naud had bowed before his wish.

"I don't know how to thank you, superintendent. I haven't behaved toward you as I should have . . ."

"You have treated me extremely well and I've shared some excellent meals with you."

"Will you tell my brother-in-law . . ."

"Of course I will! Oh! One piece of advice, if I may be so bold . . . Don't be too hard on your daughter . . ."

A fatherly flicker of a smile made Maigret realize that Naud understood perhaps far more than one might suppose.

"You're a good sort, superintendent . . . You really are! . . . I am so grateful . . ."

"You'll be grateful for the rest of your days, as a friend of mine used to say . . . Good-bye! . . . Send me a note from time to time . . ."

He walked away from the house which now seemed stilled, leaving the light behind him. Smoke rose from but two or three chimneys in the village, only to disappear into the fog. The dairy was working at full capacity and looked like a factory from a distance. Meanwhile, old Désiré was steering his boat laden with pitchers of milk along the canal.

Madame Retailleau would undoubtedly be asleep now, and the tiny postmistress too . . . Josaphat would be sleeping off his wine, and . . .

Right up to the last minute, Maigret was terrified he would bump into Louis. The lad had put so much faith in him and on discovering the superintendent had left would doubtless think to himself bitterly:

"He was one of them, too!"

Or else:

"They got the better of him!"

If they *had* got the better of him, they hadn't done so with money or fine words, at any rate.

And as he stood at the end of the platform waiting for the train and keeping an eye on his suitcase beside him, he mumbled to himself:

"Look here, son, I wish the world could be clean and beautiful, just like you . . . And I get upset and angry when . . ."

Surprise, surprise! Cavre walked on to the platform and stood about fifty yards away from the superintendent.

"That fellow, there, for instance . . . He's a scoundrel . . . He is capable of all number of dirty tricks . . . I know this for a fact . . . And yet I feel rather sorry for him . . . I've worked with him . . . I know his kind and what torments he goes through . . . What would have been the point of condemning Etienne Naud? And would he have been found guilty, anyway? . . . There is no concrete proof . . . The whole case would have stirred up a lot of dirt . . . Geneviève would have been called to the witness box . . . And Alban would not just have been worried. He would probably have been really pleased to be rid of his responsibilities . . ."

There was no sign of Louis, which was just as well, for in spite of everything Maigret was not proud of himself. This early morning departure of his smacked too much of an escape.

"You will understand later on . . . They *are* strong, as you say . . . They stick together . . ."

Having noticed Maigret, Justin Cavre came over to where he was standing but did not dare open a conversation.

"Do you hear, Cavre? I've been talking to myself, like an old . . ."

"Have you any news?"

"What sort of news? The girl is all right now. The father and mother . . . I don't like you, Cavre . . . I pity you, but I don't like you . . . It cannot be helped . . . There are some people you warm to and others you don't . . . But I am going to tell you something . . . There is one expression in common parlance that I hate more than any other. It makes me wince and grind my teeth whenever I hear it . . . Do you know what it is?"

"No."

"*It will be all right in the end!*"

The train came into the station and in the growing din Maigret shouted:

"But it *will* be all right in the end, you'll see . . ."

———

Two years later, in fact, he discovered by chance that Alban Groult-Cotelle had married Mademoiselle Geneviève Naud in Argentina, where her father had started a huge cattle-rearing concern.

"Tough luck on our friend Albert, wasn't it, Louis? But some poor devil had to be the scapegoat!"

Saint-Mesmin-Le-Vieux, March 3, 1943